WAYWARD MOON

SOULS OF THE ROAD - 2

DEVON MONK

ODD
HOUSE
PRESS

To my family - and all the dreamers on the road

ACKNOWLEDGMENTS

Pulling this book together took the efforts of many wonderful people. My heartfelt thanks goes out to the divine artist: Ravven for creating this amazing cover. That sign is perfect, and naming it the Twilight Motel still makes me laugh.

Sharon Elaine Thompson, you are a rock star copy editor and an even better friend. Thank you for coming to my rescue, and with such speed. I can't wait to hear the adventures of your own trip down Route 66 soon.

To Dejsha Knight, who has been my bulletproof beta reader for every project including this one, you are so awesome in every way. Thank you for pointing out where the wheels fell off the story.

To my husband Russ, and sons, Kameron and Konner, I love you all. You are the best parts of this drive down the road of life.

Big smooches to the Traveling Rats and assorted beloved Rodents! Let's go chase another horizon soon!

Lastly, to you, my dear readers. Thank you for taking time out of your busy lives to ramble down this old magic road with Lula and Brogan. It just wouldn't be the same without you.

Until we meet again–happy reading, and safe travels!

CHAPTER ONE

The living world carried a hell of a wallop for a guy who had been dead as long as I had been. The noise, the heat, the constant roar of people—moving, shouting, pushing, touching, talking—

"—I like graveyards," Lula Gauge, my wife, my love, was cheerfully carrying on the conversation I'd dropped. "You know I do, Brogan. All these years sleeping in them?" She drove the truck to the end of the thrift shop's empty gravel lot, parking under the fragrant shade of a mimosa tree.

I tightened my fingers in our dog, Lorde's, black fur, trying to borrow her calm as she napped between us. Her breathing was even, softened by sleep, content in this world.

Dogs, I had always believed, had life figured out.

I, on the other hand, couldn't seem to get a handle on it. It had been one month since the god, Cupid, had snapped his fingers and made me mostly alive again. He wanted us to track down people he was looking for and a book we'd run across. A book that had almost gotten us killed.

Well, more killed.

He wanted other things too. It didn't sit right with me, us being under the thumb of a god.

"Hey, handsome."

I must have been quiet too long. Again.

Lu reached across Lorde and rested her fingers on my hand. If she noticed my wince at the contact, she didn't do anything to show it.

She was sunlight, my Lu. Red hair caught in a wild tangle around her pale, pale shoulders that used to freckle good and hard before we'd both been attacked by monsters we still hadn't found.

Monsters that had made Lu a *thrawan*—that step between being human and a vampire. Monsters who had made me an earthbound spirit, and who had ripped off pieces of our souls, leaving us neither quite alive nor fully dead.

"I know—" I startled at the volume of my voice. I swallowed, and for the hundredth time, the thousandth time, reminded myself that I was solid now, that I had a voice now. "I know you don't mind graveyards. But all these years sneaking into them just to speak to you, just to touch you…"

She opened her fingers so I could thread our hands together. She waited, silent, because she was made that way. Quiet as the fire sleeping in the heart of coal.

"Brogan," she began, soft and low, a hunter soothing the trapped animal. "I think we should…"

"Hotel," I interrupted too loudly. Loud enough even Lorde woofed in her sleep.

Lu's eyebrows rose above her sunglasses.

"Hotel?"

"With a shower and fresh, soft sheets. A window with nice dark curtains."

Quiet, I thought. It would be a place for Lu to rest, a soft place. She'd spent too many years in the back of one truck or another, driving the old Route 66, or on the hard grounds of graveyards, roughing it just to be near me for scant seconds.

I hadn't said any of that out loud, but her other hand lifted, fingers finding and tracing the magic pocket watch that hung from a heavy chain beneath the edge of her yellow tank top.

"You don't like hotels." Lu's hand fell away from the watch and her fingers hooked the bottom of the steering wheel. "Too many dead and other such linger there."

"Sure," I said amiably. "But there's hot showers, soft sheets, and doors that lock. I like all those things more than I dislike a ghost or two."

"But you hate ghosts. You've never met a single one you've liked."

"I've also never met one I couldn't ignore."

She bit her bottom lip thinking. I watched her, because, how could I not? The line between her brows, the clench of her hand on the old truck's wheel told me she was worried. Worried more than she should be.

"Hey, love," I squeezed her fingers gently. "I'm still new to this breathing thing. Maybe a soft bed wouldn't be such a bad idea for a day or two?"

She wasn't convinced, but I knew how to wrangle her interest.

"Let's make a bet on it. Whoever finds the most valuable item in this thrift shop gets to choose where we sleep. I win, it's a hotel. You win, it's a graveyard."

"Or the back of Silver," she said. "All the stars above us."

"Or the back of the truck—"

"—Silver," she insisted.

"—Silver," I said, even though I still thought it was a terrible name for the old Chevy. "All those mosquitoes around us."

She tipped her head down, her eyes, gold like autumn honey, peering over the top of her sunglasses. "I love you," she said. This, her forever vow.

"I love you, Lula." This, my forever answer.

"But you are gonna lose that bet," she said.

I chuckled, and the feelings wedged behind my breastbone broke up and lifted away.

"You think you're going to win?" I asked.

"Yep."

"Against me?"

"I have spent decades on this road, Brogan Gauge."

"So have I."

"But I've spent them finding magical items. Items that I've sold to the highest bidder."

I knew all this. I'd been with her every step of the way, even if she hadn't always seen me. "Sure, but Headwaters will buy anything you wave under their nose."

"His, I think," she said. "His nose."

We'd never met the mysterious antique collector with a thirst for arcane and magical items. We didn't care who they were as long as the money was deposited into the bank on time.

"My point is," she said, "I know a valuable thing when I see one. A magical thing."

"That so?" The deep burr in my voice made her focus on me. It was a beautiful thing being the full focus of that woman. "I know a valuable thing when I see one too," I said. "The most valuable thing worth living for."

I lifted her hand to my lips and pressed a soft kiss on the back of her cool fingers, holding eye contact the whole time.

The glitter of tears surprised me.

"I've missed you," she whispered, and I didn't know if I should let go of her hand or pull her closer.

Emotions were difficult and mostly snuck up on me unexpected. Maybe on her too. Neither of us were navigating the change as well as we wanted.

I pulled her toward me. "Lu, I—"

She tugged her hand away and sniffed. "Oh, no. None of that sappy stuff. You can't distract me with sweetness, Brogan Gauge." Her voice wasn't quite steady, but almost.

Almost happy. Almost light.

She unlatched her seatbelt, rolled down the window a few inches, and opened the door. "I have a bet to win."

She slipped down out of the cab, closing the door behind her.

Lorde lifted her head and tracked Lu strolling around the front of the truck.

"You stay here, girl," I said with one last stroke over her silky ears. She shook her head then settled back to napping.

I rolled down the window, so Lorde had plenty of fresh air, and stepped out of the truck.

Missouri's early morning yawned, hot and sticky. If the lackluster wind was any sign, it was going to turn out to be a real scorcher.

"We each find one valuable item we can sell," Lu reminded me, as if she had to. "You're buying a pair of jeans."

"My trousers are fine." We sauntered toward the shop door, kicking up dust, the taste of gravel hitting the back of my tongue. Lu threw me a side-eye, and I worked on not wincing with each step.

My old wool trousers might be fine, but my new shoes were not.

"And a new pair of shoes."

"My shoes are also fine," I lied. I opened the door, setting off a clunker of a bell, glanced in the cluttered interior, then held the door open for her.

Lu slipped her sunglasses onto the top of her head and stepped past me. "Your shoes are too small because you didn't try them on before you bought them."

"I know the size of my feet," I grumbled, but she was already gone, cutting straight toward a rack of clothing.

I took a breath, smelled mustiness, dust, and weirdly, dill, then plunged into the space after her. I did one lap around the shop to check for dangers out of habit, then paused by the checkout counter set in the far corner so it had a good view of the shop and the door.

The old man there had to be ninety if he was a day, his eyes glassy with cataracts, his hair a wispy afterthought behind liver-spotted ears. I was pretty sure the only light at the end of his tunnel was the glint off the Grim Reaper's scythe.

"You're one of them, aren't you?" The old timer's voice creaked there at the end, but was strong enough to carry over the garbling noise of the thrift shop's speaker system plowing its way through hits from fifty years ago.

I raised my eyebrows and stuffed one hand in my pocket, aiming to look less intimidating. Added a slouch to knock a few inches off my six-feet four and tipped my shoulders so they seemed more narrow.

I was a big man and knew the assumptions folks made about me.

"I'm not one of anything," I said. "Except passing through."

His sour expression didn't change, but his knotted knuckles tightened over the modern cell phone he'd set on the counter in front of him. "I know the sheriff. I'll call you in. The both of you. I don't need no trouble with the Riggs or the Kearneys. I run a clean establishment."

"Clean…" The floor had been swept, but whoever had done it hadn't bothered to do more than push dirt and debris against the walls. The windows were edged with a yellow smudge and crammed with stacks of suitcases and Mason jars filled with dirt. The shelves leaned at exhausted angles behind tables heaped with junk.

I frowned at the display of more canning jars behind him, all of those were filled with dirt too. The smell of dill was stronger here as was a hint of mint.

Clean was not the word I'd use to describe The Big Hunt Thrift and Junk.

"Riggs and Kearneys live around here?" I asked easy and low. "They giving you trouble?"

"I said I'll call the sheriff." He held my gaze, and I decided he'd served in a war or two.

"No need for the sheriff. We're just shopping is all. My wife and I." I tipped my head toward Lula, who was pushing hangers from one side of a rack to the other, listening, but not interfering yet. I supposed she was hoping I'd learned my lesson from the disastrous gas station stop in Fenton and wouldn't let this get out of hand this time.

"Those Riggs," I said, "they a gang?"

He blinked, and for the first time since I'd walked in, the anger rolling off him shifted to something else. Confusion.

"Not…well, I suppose… No. They're related though. A family."

"And they look like me?"

His gaze took me in, mostly the height, the width, as I didn't think he could actually make out my dark hair or the color of my eyes.

"No, though they don't all look the same, no matter what they are."

"And what are they?"

His mouth folded back into deep wrinkles. "You wouldn't believe me if I said."

"Might." I waited. Despite what Lu thought, I could be patient. Had spent all of these years patient. Too many years.

"They're monsters."

The truth put a hard snap in his voice, bitter because he knew no one would believe him. He knew I wouldn't believe him.

But I knew monsters were real.

After all, I was one. Come to that, so was Lu.

Lu stopped pushing the hangers, the steady squeak of metal-on-metal silent now.

"All right," I said, hoping he'd tell me more. We were looking for some monsters ourselves. Looking to kill the ones who had cursed us to decades of half-living.

I ducked so he would meet my gaze, wanting him to see I believed. "Do you know what kind of monster?"

"Of course I know," he said. "Do you?"

The dull clink of the bell over the door pulled his attention, breaking the moment.

A middle-aged woman with a poof of brown hair cut in a bob and four teen girls single-filed into the shop, all of them arguing about a song I'd never heard.

The old guy took that as his cue to step away from the cash register. He messed with the bags of generic candy pegged on a shelf, angling to keep an eye on the women.

Whatever he knew, he wasn't going to tell it to me now.

I made my way to Lu, who was sliding hangers again, acting like she hadn't heard the entire thing.

"You're whistling," she said, not looking up.

"Am I?" I was. Making my own noise was one way to combat the chatter of the teens, the scuff and squeak of so many shoes across the chipped linoleum, the sudden explosions of laughter that made me jerk.

"Nat King Cole," she informed me as hangers *snick, snick, snick*ed.

I didn't know how she was always so relaxed. She tugged a shirt off the rack, and draped it over the others in her arms, the fluid shift of her muscle under skin, the smell of her perfume, deep rose and sweetness, familiar as my own heartbeat.

I wanted her always. All the time. Forever.

I inhaled, exhaled, and tried to wiggle my toes to release my stress. Since my shoes were about two sizes too tight, it didn't help.

"That so?"

She nodded.

I turned my back to the row of shirts behind her and crossed my arms.

"It's that song about the enchanted boy looking for the greatest thing," she said.

"Mmmm?"

"You know the words," she said.

"Might."

She glanced down the length of the rack. I savored her profile, the twitch of her lips as she tried not to smile at me.

I was smiling at her. Because how could I not?

"What is the greatest thing?" I asked.

"Brogan."

"Well, of course. I'm *one* of the greatest things, but certainly not the *only* greatest thing to sing about."

She huffed a short laugh, and I moved toward her, crowding up into her space, wanting to catch her happiness like a wish in the air. Wanting to be the one who made her feel that way.

"The song isn't about you." She added another shirt to the others over her arm.

"No?" I slid my hand under the pile of clothes she was holding, finding her fingers there and slotting mine between them. "Then what's the greatest thing in all the world that the poor boy in the song is searching for?"

She lifted her gaze to mine, and I knew what coal felt like right before the match hit.

"Love," she said. "The greatest thing is to love."

"And to be loved." I tugged her hand, wanting her closer, needing to kiss her.

She swayed, just a little, and I couldn't look away from the gold, gold, gold of her eyes.

Then she dumped the heap of clothes into my arms and shoved my shoulder. "Try them on. Especially the jeans. It's too hot for wool."

I blinked, frowned. "But…"

"Dressing room." She pointed toward a shower stall at the back of the shop. "And you still haven't found something valuable."

"But…"

"Are you giving up on our bet already?" She was walking backward, her eyes still on me, that smile gone wide now.

I smirked. "Oh, not a chance."

She made big eyes. "Then you better shake a leg, hot shot. Clothes first."

"I have enough clothing."

"Jeans." She pointed one more time, then spun and put that sway in her hips that always got me wanting.

When Cupid had snapped me back into the living world, he'd snapped me with my clothes on. While I appreciated it, wearing wool in summer in Missouri was like walking around in a wet, hot blanket full of leeches. All wool trousers had done so far was remind me why the civilized world had moved on to other materials.

Like cotton.

Maybe Lu was right. Maybe I needed new clothes.

I clomped off to the changing room. I didn't see the need to try clothing on, but this was only the second time I'd bought anything since coming back to the living world. That first time I'd gotten my shoe size wrong, and the shirts I'd blindly grabbed off the rack were too tight in the arms.

The changing room was a particle board closet with a mustard shower curtain on a rod. I stepped in, closed the curtain and rested my back against the back of the closet, my shoulders almost touching either wall.

I closed my eyes and swallowed the edge of panic, letting the tightness in my chest and stomach shudder through me.

It was a lot, this world. Most days it was more than I could handle.

But I didn't want Lu to know that. Didn't want her to think I wasn't strong enough to be at her side.

"This is how life's always been, Brogan," I whispered. "You wanted this. You begged for this. So you better damn well get used to it."

I inhaled, held the breath, focusing on the stretch of lungs, the soft drumming of my heart. The woman and teens were laughing, all of them too loud. One of them dared another to try something on, which they must have done, if the wild cackling indicated anything.

The old guy at the cash register was rustling empty hangers in the box beneath the counter, making sure we all knew we were being watched.

And Lu...well, Lu was sunlight pulling me heavenward.

I heard her footsteps, always light, as if she were dancing through this life. Heard her fingers pushing hangers again. She considered something, decided against it, and her steps moved farther into the store, back to where shadow and dust collected.

Back where she'd probably find some rare antique or magical item and win the damn bet while her shell-shocked husband hid in a changing room.

"No you don't, Lula Gauge." I opened my eyes and blew out a breath. "I want a shower tonight. I want a soft damn bed. That means hotel. That means I'm winning this bet."

I tossed the pile of clothes on the folding chair, made quick work of pulling the sleeves of the shirts over my arms, but didn't bother with the buttons.

"Blue works, don't like the other two button downs, and who cares how tight or loose a T-shirt fits? No one cares. I'm not trying them on."

"Are you arguing with your clothes?" Lu had circled back and was standing right outside the changing room.

"Almost done," I said, embarrassed I hadn't noticed I was thinking out loud. I'd done so much of it when I was a spirit, it was hard to remember to keep my mouth shut.

"The jeans. You're not leaving without a pair."

"A man can dress himself," I grouched.

"Not when a man thinks wool in August makes sense."

"The wool fits." I toed off the shoes that jammed my toenails. I dropped trouser. The rush of muggy air against my bare skin was absolute heaven, and I tried not to groan in relief.

"You'll like the cut of the denim," she said.

"Pants are pants, Lu." I tugged on the blue denim, zipped, buttoned. "Huh."

"Well?"

"Well what?"

"Do you like them?"

I shoved the curtain to one side. "Pants are pants…" The rest of whatever smartass thing I was about to say died on my lips.

Lu liked what she saw. From the heat in her eyes and the pink splash across her cheeks, she very much liked looking at me, shirtless, shoeless, in nothing but a pair of jeans.

"But these are *good* pants," she almost purred.

I couldn't help it. I gave her a wink. "That so?"

"Mmm-hmm."

"They fit how they should?" I asked, holding my

arms out to the side as far as the changing room would allow, shamelessly giving her the gold-ticket show, not wanting her eyes on anyone but me.

She took that one step closer, every line of her body gone from playful to predator. "I like them."

"That so?" My throat had gone dry, and the words sort of crackled up and blew away.

"But I love the man in them." She came to a stop, placing her cool fingers on my left hip, right above the denim waistband.

That smallest amount of skin on skin was shocking, thrilling.

I swallowed. "Well." I swallowed again. "Isn't that something?"

"It is," she said not moving closer, but somehow making my skin go even hotter.

I was absolutely wordless.

"Buy them." She tugged on the belt loop, and I missed the cool pressure of her fingertips. Missed that solid, real contact. Missed being reminded I was alive and she was alive and there were a whole lot of things we could do to celebrate that. "Put on your shirt first. You're making a scene."

She pointed to the left, her motion hidden from anyone else because she kept her hand between us.

I reluctantly looked that way and found two of the teenagers staring openly at me. The woman with them caught my gaze and blushed. She tapped one of the girls, breaking the spell, and shooed them down the aisle.

I gave the woman a big smile. She shrugged and

rolled her eyes at the girls, like what-are-you-going-to-do before she found a sweater that suddenly needed her attention.

"Well," I said. "Looks like you're not the only one enjoying the show." I tucked my thumbs in the belt loops and leaned one shoulder on the doorframe. The whole closet creaked and leaned.

Lu shook her head. "Nope. This," she waved her finger in a circle, encompassing the all of me, "is *my* show. Got that, Brogan Gauge?"

My heart hammered approval at her possessive tone. "One hundred percent."

"So now?" she asked, eyebrows raising.

"So now I'm gonna buy some jeans."

"Good." She stepped back, and it took what strength and decency I had not to reach out and drag her into this wobbly little closet and show her just how much she was mine.

She nodded one more time, her gaze tracking all over me like she was taking notes on where she wanted to put her lips and teeth. I took it as the promise it was.

I pulled the curtain shut and swiftly tried on the other jeans. They buttoned and zipped. Good enough.

I got back in my clothes, shoved my feet into the tight shoes with a grunt, then opened the curtain again.

Lu was gone.

CHAPTER TWO

I scanned the shop, looking for my wife. Over the muddy speaker system, poor Frank Sinatra was trying to fly to the moon, and it sounded like he was doing it in a snorkel.

A flash of red hair between the shelves of kitchenware caught my eye, then Lu crouched.

Knowing her, she'd found the most valuable item in the store trapped under the waffle irons.

"No, you don't," I muttered. "You are not going to win this bet."

I strode to the checkout, dropped the shirts and jeans on the end, and nodded at the old fellow. "I'll take these. But there's a couple other things I want too."

He opened his mouth.

"I'm paying cash."

He closed his mouth. Money was money, and almost no one drove down this particular abandoned stretch of Route 66 anymore. I knew. I'd been driving it for nearly a hundred years.

I shouldered my way toward the back of the store, intending to win.

"Not clothing," I said to myself, as I did a perimeter of the shop. "Wouldn't know the value of an old coat if it was printed on the collar. Something else. She's already gone through the collectibles. Keeping me busy trying on clothes so she could get a step ahead. Clever.

"What wouldn't you have checked, Lu? What would you overlook?"

I was staring at a rusted file cabinet, half a set of bent golf clubs, and an electric heater when it hit me.

I whistled my way across the store, nice and casual-like. Lu popped her head up over a stack of old table-cloths, her gaze tracking me.

I grinned and gave her a little wave.

She squinted.

I made like I was interested in a pile of postcards to buy time.

Turned out the postcards were pretty interesting, some of them old enough I thought they'd be worth picking up for sale to a local collector. I sorted out five in the best shape and then, when I was pretty sure Lu wasn't watching any more, I moseyed over to the books.

It was a risk. Most people didn't know a valuable book when they had their hands on one.

Books were fragile, easily destroyed. But they were a compulsion for me. I liked them. Back when I had been living, I'd done what I could to learn as much as possible about what made one rare.

I dragged my finger across some older hardbacks

and tugged at a few of the smaller volumes. I needed to find something better, worth more than whatever my shark of a wife was tracking down.

The books weren't older than the early fifties, and none of them were collectible. I was about to turn away when I spotted a little gold bookmark tossed in with some hat pins, several broken watches, and a silver sewing kit.

Easy money would be the silver sewing kit. It was intact except for the original thimble, so I picked that up.

But it was the little bookmark that was my ticket to the motel hot shower of my dreams. The bottom of it was shaped like a trowel with a break in it for sliding over a page.

The top was a woman's hand holding a crystal ball. That little bookmark was magic. Enough magic, I hesitated to touch it.

"It's just a little magic," I whispered, wiping the sweat off my forehead with my arm. "Nothing to be afraid of, Brogan. Magic, magic like this, won't do you harm. Pick it up, pay, and collect that hot shower."

I knew I was being ridiculous. I wasn't afraid of magic. But I couldn't force my hand forward, couldn't make my fingers do as I said.

Magic, some kind or other, had carved a piece of my soul out of me and deposited it in Lu. Magic, some kind or other, had done the same to her.

Magic wielded by a powerful monster we had yet to kill.

And now, magic wielded by a god had given me a place back in the living world.

No matter how I tried to convince myself that magic in small doses couldn't do those sorts of things that destroyed a man's life, a part of me knew magic was magic: destructive no matter what size package it came in.

The bell above the door let out one small clank.

I waited for the second clunk indicating the door had closed, but after an extended silence, I lifted my head.

A girl stood in the doorway. Her hair was thistle-down white and silvery blue, bunched in waves below her ears and chopped into heavy bangs above her eyes. Her face was round, soft, her frame stocky.

I placed her at eight, maybe nine, her clothing layers of color: purple leggings beneath a loose blue dress over green sandals.

But it was her eyes that caught me. They were dark, large, and frightened, darting quickly from one side to the other as if she expected danger from every corner.

As if she expected harm.

I straightened, leaving the bookmark where it was, and moved out into the aisle. I was closer to the back of the shop than the door. I might not be as fast as I'd been as an undead, but if anything came at her, I could reach her quickly, pull her out of the way, shield her.

The teens in the back of the shop squealed at something they'd found. The girl in the doorway flinched and pulled the hand that wasn't holding the door up in a fist against her chest.

Her gaze was everywhere again, before it settled on me.

Even in the grimy light, those eyes were a brown so deep, I felt like I was looking into the rich, soft shadows of a loamy forest.

"Oh," I said, an exhale of wonder.

She appeared to be a child, yes, but she was not young. A very old soul, or perhaps a very old being, stared back at me from those eyes.

Not a monster, but something that was not exactly human either.

Fae, angel, or some other magical creature? Why did I feel as if I knew her, as if she were as familiar as day and night?

Before I could gather any kind of answer, the man behind the cash register caught sight of the girl.

"Out!" he shouted. "I've told you before. Out of my shop."

She startled again, this time her gaze landing quickly on the old man's face, then the phone he held aloft like a grenade he was about to pull the pin out of.

She rocked back, body poised to flee, but hesitated. The fear on her was palpable. I could almost see the fast beating of her heart from here. But just when I thought she'd scurry off, she settled her shoulders and tipped her whole body back toward the open doorway.

"My backpack," she said, and there was an accent to it I couldn't place. "Dan left my backpack here."

The man scowled. "I don't need your trouble. I don't need your lies. Go."

"He left it," the girl insisted, the toes of one foot

sliding over the threshold, most of her still outside. "He left it here."

"If it was left here, it's mine now."

I opened my mouth, but Lu beat me to it. "What does it look like?"

The girl inhaled. She didn't breathe for the few seconds it took Lu to walk closer to her. Again I thought she'd run.

Lu left plenty of room between them, several feet. "The backpack," Lu said. "What does it look like?"

"She's not welcome here," the man said.

I'd had enough. I strode to the counter and used my height and bulk to my advantage. "How about you leave her alone and ring up my purchases?"

The old man stood his ground—I had to give him credit for that. But he didn't hold that ground for long.

"She's not welcome in my shop," he said.

"I heard. As you can see, she's not in the shop. She's in the doorway."

He glared at me, and color crept up his face under the mottle of liver spots and veins. I wondered if he was going to yell or finally use that phone of his to call the sheriff.

I opened my wallet and thumbed out a few twenties, showing him there was more than enough.

That, finally, put his foot on the gas. He got busy ringing up the clothing and postcards, and I stayed right there, looming over him, putting myself between him and the girl in the doorway.

Lu made a quick once-through the shop, looking for the girl's backpack, but I had another idea.

"You have a lost and found?"

"No." His eyes cut to the side and down. There was something down there.

"Let me ask that again while I'm feeling charitable. How about you let me see the lost and found you keep below the counter?"

"I don't have her damn bag," he growled.

"Good. Then I don't expect to see it when you pull the lost and found up from under the counter."

"I don't owe you *people* anything." He wadded the last pair of jeans and shoved them in a plastic bag with red writing on it that looked like it'd come from a Chinese food restaurant. "You should mind your own business and stay away from her kind."

I glanced at the door and found the girl staring at me. Her night-shadow eyes were wide and liquid.

Hopeful. She looked hopeful.

Lu set a little statue of a rabbit, the magical bookmark, and a small blue backpack on the counter. "Add these to the total, please."

I dropped another twenty on the counter with slow, purposeful motion.

"We *people*," I said, putting the emphasis in the same place he had, "have no quarrels with you." I released the edge of the bill so that it snapped softly. "If you want it to stay that way, keep your judgement to yourself."

The man narrowed his eyes, but wisely kept his mouth shut.

I leaned away from the counter, gathered up the bag and loose items, and dropped my free hand to my side.

Before I knew it, Lu's palm was there, just like it always was.

I pressed my hand against hers. Just as I always would.

CHAPTER THREE

The girl in the doorway watched Lu and me walk toward her. Her eyes dropped to the backpack in my hand only once, then flicked back up.

Strangely, her gaze locked on Lu. Most people would assume I was the bigger threat, just from the size of me.

But this girl— No, she was something more than a girl. This *being* watched Lu, liquid eyes wide and frightened, every muscle in her tuned tight as a harp string.

As if Lu were the threat instead of the huge man beside her. Maybe she was right. Lu could take care of herself and me. Had done so for almost a hundred years.

"All right now," I said, as we reached the door. "Step outside, please. Let's give this man his rightful space."

Her nostrils quivered a second, maybe a twitch, maybe she was scenting me, scenting us. She bit her top lip, sucking it under her teeth. Then she blew out a breath and took big, backward steps, not turning away, her eyes still wary.

"Is this your backpack?" I asked.

She blinked. Nodded.

"We'll give it to you. We just want to know your name. And if you're okay."

Lu tipped her head, hearing it before I did. The soft sound of feet in the dry grass, the measured breathing waiting, waiting. We were not alone out here. Nor were we the only monsters.

"I'm Ra—I'm Abbi," the girl said. She pulled a flower out of her pocket, just a little wild thing with yellow petals, and picked at the stem, slowly snipping off bits with her fingernails. "I'm okay, but I think I need a ride."

"She doesn't need a ride," a woman's voice said from the ramble of weeds that butted up to the parking lot.

The werewolves were not a surprise. We were in their territory, had been since we crossed from St. Louis to Gray Summit. But I was surprised at how many were here. Six I could see, another six scattered in the tall grass and trees beyond the lot.

The speaker was strong, old enough to have silver popping through her dark, spiky hair.

"That so?" I asked. "What's Abbi got to say about that?"

The woman narrowed her eyes, then held her hand out for Abbi. "She has nothing to say. Abbi. Come."

Abbi finally looked away from Lu and squared her shoulders. She walked toward me with a kind of drifting grace I wouldn't have expected from a girl that young, and stopped right in front of me.

"Abbi," the woman said. A warning. Frustration. She took one step forward, the other werewolves shifting at her movement.

"Not yet, Summer," Abbi said.

I tensed to put myself between the pack and the girl, but the woman, Summer, stopped, and so did the others. From the tilt of her hips and her fingers in a loose fist, she wasn't angry, just annoyed.

"You found my backpack," Abbi said.

"Lu found it." I held it out for her.

"You bought it for me."

"Sure," I said, like it was nothing. I held very still, working to make my body language show my awareness of the werewolves, protectiveness of Lu, and worry for the girl.

From the tension in Lu, being unalive had not improved my ability to be subtle.

The werewolves could probably see the fight in me, and I knew Lu itched to pull a dagger, just so they knew whoever tried to touch me would bleed.

"Can I have it?" Abbi asked.

"Of course."

She smiled so bright, her whole face lit up.

The werewolves relaxed slightly.

"Thank you." She shrugged it on and looked over at Lu again. "You found it."

"Yes, I did."

"You're good at finding things."

It was a statement, but I had most of my attention

on the group of shifters behind her. They didn't like this line of questioning. I wondered why.

"Sometimes," Lu said. "Some things."

"Magic things?"

"Sometimes."

"Can you find something for me? Help find something for me?"

"Abbi," Summer warned. "We don't need them."

"Is she a part of your pack?" I asked the wolf. Abbi wasn't distressed, but it was clear they didn't like her talking to us. "Is she family?"

Summer strolled forward, strength radiating off her. If she wasn't the head of the pack, the Alpha, she was in very high standing. Two men moved forward out of the tall grass to stand at either side behind her. One had eyes the color of chipped glaciers.

"She belongs," Summer said.

I wasn't sure what that meant.

"Do you need a safe place?" I asked Abbi.

Abbi's face scrunched up and her nostrils twitched. She didn't look away from Lu though. "I am safe with them. Summer and Danube and all of them. They love me."

The man I thought might be Danube, who was standing beside Summer, snorted.

"They do," Abbi insisted. "They worship me."

I flicked a gaze at Summer, and she met mine with a bemused expression.

"Worship is going a little far, don't you think?" she said.

"Oh, no. You all love me. It's why you think you're looking after me."

"We *are* looking after you," said the man with those blue, blue eyes.

Summer lifted her hand to warn him to silence. He huffed and crossed his arms over his chest.

"We don't trust strangers, Abbi," Summer said.

Abbi rolled her eyes and mouthed *werewolves*. "They aren't strangers now, are they? They know my name and their names are…"

"Lu and Brogan," Lu said.

Abbi smiled. "Lu and Brogan. You're not afraid of the dark are you?"

Every werewolf tightened. Several growled softly.

"No one's afraid of the dark," Lu said softly. "Just the things hiding in it."

Abbi nodded and nodded. "There are Shadows in the dark. Lost Shadows. Someone needs to find them. My Shadow—"

The door clunked open, and I knew without turning that the shopkeeper was there.

"Loitering is a misdemeanor punishable by fines and community service," the old man said. "I have 911 on speed dial and happen to know the sheriff's bored today, because my son-in-law is always bored."

"We're leaving, Mr. Walch," Summer said. "Abbi."

"But—" Abbi said.

"We promised not to bother Mr. Walch anymore, remember?" Summer said.

"Yes."

"Come on, little moon."

Abbi scrunched her face, but then she sighed. "Okay. Fine." She gave Lu one more curious look. "Thank you for finding my backpack."

"You're welcome."

"Thank you for buying it," she said to me.

"My pleasure."

Abbi turned and took Summer's hand. In just a few steps the girl was ahead of her, babbling about the sky and clouds and leading Summer to a path cut through the grass.

Summer seemed perfectly content to follow her, and the four other pack members I could see fell into place behind them.

"Damn Riggs," the shop keeper muttered. "Like I need werewolves scaring all my customers away." He ducked back inside and slammed the door.

"Huh," Lu said.

"You think she's okay?" I stared at the retreating backs of the werewolves.

Abbi was almost skipping, tugging Summer forward. One of the men who had stood guard was slightly ahead of Abbi. He paused to ruffle her white hair affectionately.

She looked fine. More than fine. She looked happy.

But I was still in high-alert mode.

Lu touched my arm.

I jerked my arm away and took two steps back before I managed to put the brakes on my fight-or-flight reaction. I quickly grabbed her hand and put it back on my arm. "I didn't mean to pull away—"

"I know." She pressed her palm flat, increasing the contact. "Do you want to talk about it?"

If I never had to speak about how overwhelmed I was by the physical world, and how utterly stupid I felt when I overreacted, that'd be fine with me.

"Abbi's okay," I said.

Lu let me get away with the subject change. She squeezed my arm and leaned in toward me, inhaling, exhaling. "She looks okay."

"Are you sniffing me?"

"Why? Do you think that's strange?"

"Yes."

She eased back, a smile on her face. Before she could get away, I shifted and wrapped my arms around her, pulling her close.

"I didn't say I didn't like it," I rumbled in her ear.

She rested there a moment, warm and alive in my arms, breathing me in. If she noticed how fast my heart was beating, she didn't mention it.

"I won," she said, her words almost lost in my shirt fabric. "I found the magical item that's worth something. We're sleeping under the stars tonight."

I grunted, trying to sound annoyed, but with Lu in my arms, I found it impossible.

CHAPTER FOUR

Devil's Elbow was a lumber-chewing bend in the Big Piney River that got enough attention back in the early 1900s that the Ozark lumberjack encampment there eventually grew into an unincorporated town.

There wasn't much to it back then except the trees for logging, the river for fishing, and the forest for hunting.

But when a bridge was built across the river in 1923, a few more buildings popped up, including one that was both an inn and a sandwich shop/café.

The building had gone through floods, ownerships, and plenty of years of neglect. But it was still standing, a single-story wooden building with a gabled roof that had seen better days.

Not the worst place to stop for an early lunch.

Country music laid a low, soothing vibe over the darkened dining area. The half dozen people at the bar were arguing over some reality show playing on the TV that involved survival.

Lu sat with her back to the door, so I was facing it. She thumbed through something on her phone, her lunch of french fries largely ignored.

I'd devoured a pile of brisket and was drinking water, trying to decide if I should go for the chicken and a beer. A headache pricked behind my eyes, hard enough I jabbed a thumb above my eyebrow, trying to relieve it.

"Asshole like you doesn't even know how lucky he is," a man's voice said from behind me.

I turned, frowning into the darkened room.

"If I were alive, I wouldn't sit there and let her scroll through dating sites."

There was no one behind me. No one over my right shoulder, which is where I thought I'd heard the voice. I twisted to get a better look over my left shoulder.

The headache spiked, then my vision snapped.

I could see him.

A ghost.

Just what I needed.

This one was a man, tall and lean in life, dark, messy hair, scruff that might have been an anchor style goatee, or might have been he didn't know how to shave properly.

He wore a white T-shirt with a leather vest over it, ripped jeans, and boots, and all of him was outlined in a moon-silver light. Next to him was a huge wolf, also outlined in silver.

The wolf turned its head toward me, and its eyes flashed red.

"I'd take her someplace nicer than this crapfest, that's for damn sure. You know who has good barbecue? Texas."

"Then go haunt Texas," I muttered.

His head snapped my way, eyes flashing red. "You *can* hear me. Sonofabitch. I thought you were blind *and* deaf."

I sighed and rubbed my head, although the headache was gone now.

Lu's thumb paused on the side of her phone. "Texas?"

"Ghost."

She looked to both sides. I tipped my thumb to my left. "Big mouth. Bad fashion choices."

The ghost, to my surprise, laughed. "Asshole."

"Problem?" Lu asked.

"Nope."

She glared in the ghost's general direction, then went back to her phone.

"So, it's been awhile since anyone has talked to me," he said.

"Nope."

"I haven't even asked you anything yet."

I drank the rest of my water ignoring him.

"Come on, pal. Just give me a few minutes of your time. I know things. Things you want to hear."

Since every ghost I'd encountered from the day I'd died said the same thing, I didn't respond. Ghosts were a little like used car salespeople. The less eye contact, the better chance of getting out of the situation un-accosted.

"No, don't ignore me. Do you know how long I've been dead? You're the first Sighted I've met. I have things to say."

He stormed around to stand behind Lu, then bent down right next to her, his cheek almost touching hers. She pulled to one side, away from him, her eyebrows raised.

"What?" he asked, watching me watching him. "You don't want me to touch her?" He pointed a finger at her and moved it closer to her face.

Lu put her hand up by her cheek. "Is he next to me?"

"Yep."

"Doing something annoying?"

"Not for long." I pushed my chair out and wondered if I could still kick a ghost's ass.

But before I could slap the boo-shit outta the guy, the door opened, and Cupid strolled in.

Lu stilled at the same moment I did, both of us feeling that deep resonant hum of power that was unique to gods.

"Bo," I said, so she didn't have to turn around to see which god was coming our way.

"Holy crap, you can see gods too?" the ghost asked. "What *are* you?"

Lu stood and brought her chair over to sit next to me.

Cupid, who liked to go by Bo, didn't even look at us. I knew it couldn't be a coincidence he was here, in

Devil's Elbow, in this bar, exactly when Lu and I had decided to get some food.

"Do you know that god?" the ghost asked. "I've never met that one."

Lu dragged her plate across the table toward her and dipped a fry in ketchup before biting it in half.

I spun my empty water glass between my fingers and wished I'd ordered that beer.

The ghost came round the table and stood at my left.

"This god after you?" he asked. "Did you do something to piss him off? Because I am so here for this. You want to fight a god? I'll help you fight a god."

"I don't want your help to fight a god," I said.

"Maybe," Lu interrupted. "Maybe we'd want your help, but not yet."

"She can see me?"

"Nope."

"But she trusts me?"

"Nope."

"Did you call Bo?" Lu asked.

"No."

"Did he?"

I glanced over at the lanky spirit. "You lying?"

"Not today."

"Did you call Cupid?"

"That's Cupid?" The ghost looked the burley god up and down. "I thought Cupid was a baby angel in a diaper with a cute little bow and little heart arrows."

Cupid was none of those things. He was tattooed down both arms and hands and dressed like a biker who was powering through his sixties. His head was bald, his eyes dark. A diamond winked at the top of one ear, hoops of gold shone from both lobes. His long gray goatee was topped by a handlebar mustache.

He was carrying three beers over to our table.

"Lula, Brogan," the god of connections and destruction said with a nod, "mind if I sit?"

There was a chair on the other side of the table that hadn't been there a moment before.

"Go ahead," I said.

"Beer?" He placed two in the center of the table, and I tried to remember my legends and fairy tales. Drinking with the fairy folk was never a good idea, and Persephone gave a lot up for a few pomegranate seeds. But had I ever heard the consequences of drinking with Cupid?

"Didn't expect to see you here." Lu reached for the beer, which turned into a bottle of Bludwine. She huffed a short exhale. "I haven't seen this in years. I thought it was discontinued."

"It was," Bo said.

Lu took a sip of the cherry soda, then smiled at the bottle. "It's been a long time."

Bo tipped back his own beverage, one of those craft beers I thought you could only get on tap in the Pacific Northwest.

I reached for the remaining bottle. By the time I drew it near, it had become a Hay Stack beer. I'd never heard of it, but the label said it was from some town called Ordinary, which was a dumb name for a town, if you asked me.

I swallowed a mouthful and grunted in approval. It was the best damn beer I'd ever tasted.

"Good enough?" Bo asked.

I rubbed my thumb along the label fighting the urge to drink it all in one go. "Not bad."

"Good. I need to reassess our agreement."

Lu and I tensed up, and the ghost's wolf let out a little growl. "You made a deal with a god?" the ghost asked. "How many kinds of stupid are you? You know gods and all the creatures like them are unpredictable. Vengeful. You know they ignore the people who beg them for help. Just listen to them scream and leave them to die at the bottom of some filthy cave."

The wolf snarled and took a step toward Bo.

Bo snapped his fingers.

The wolf jerked like he'd just bopped his nose against a window.

"Well, shit," the ghost breathed.

"To begin with," Bo went on like the ghost wasn't even there, like he hadn't just stopped the ghost wolf in its tracks, "I need you to tell me you remember the rules of our agreement."

"We stay alive," Lu said, "or…as alive as we are, together. You don't change that as long as we find things for you, bring people together for you, and deliver things for you."

"That's a lot," the ghost said. "You're doing everything. All his grunt work. What do you get out of this? What do you get?"

"In exchange, we have the right to break this deal at any time without consulting you."

"Oh," the ghost said. "All right. An exit plan. Not the dumbest thing to ask for."

"That's true," Bo said. "Anything else?"

"You said you'd help us find the book." Lu's finger touched the feather key under her shirt, and Bo's sharp gaze followed. "And you told us to find a rabbit. I found a small statue." She pulled the little rabbit statue out of her jacket pocket and put it on the table in front of her. "But I don't think that's it."

"It isn't," he said. "You've already found the rabbit and passed it by."

I frowned. "It's not that guy is it?" I thumbed toward the ghost, who made an affronted sound.

Bo smiled, and the diamond stud in his ear shattered light. "No, Valentine isn't a rabbit."

"Holy fuck," the ghost whispered. "You know I'm here? You know my name? You have to listen to me. I was murdered. I want revenge."

Bo took another swig of beer, then turned his full attention to the ghost.

"I am not the god of death. I am not the god of reincarnation. What you seek, I cannot give you."

"But you *are* a god." The ghost, Valentine, placed one fist on the table, leather and beads wrapped around his wrist shifting as he leaned right into Bo's space. "You can bend universes to your whim. I'll make it worth your while. I'll do what they can't do for you. I'll find your rabbit."

"No," I said, maybe a little too loudly if the sudden attention from the other patrons in the place meant anything. "No," I said quieter. "We'll find the rabbit. If

Valentine wants to make another deal with you, that's his business, but not ours, understand?"

Bo hummed. "You've already seen my rabbit and passed it by, Brogan. Our deal stands, but I am trying to help you. That was part of our bargain too. For reasons I can't divulge—sometimes even gods must tread softly —Valentine will help you to find it."

"No," I said.

"Yes!" the ghost said. "And if I do that, if I help them help you, you will owe me, god. You will *owe* me."

Bo's eyes, clear and calm, went black with storms. "I don't owe you anything. Do not test my patience."

Valentine's wolf snarled, but the ghost didn't pull back. "Or what? You'll kill me? I wonder what that would be like? Wandering around dead."

"We don't need him to help us," Lu said.

"We surely the fuck do not," I agreed.

Valentine straightened and stuck his hands under his armpits. "Screw that. I'm in. Just to get out of this place. Just to…do something. I'm in. I'll find the rabbit."

Bo nodded, pleased everything had gone his way. "Good. Brogan, Lu, find the rabbit. With Val."

I opened my mouth, but Lu put her hand over my wrist, asking me to wait.

"And then what?" she asked. "We find the rabbit. With Valentine's help. Then do we return it to you, or deliver it to someone, or to somewhere?"

"You'll know. You'll know what to do."

"That's vague, Bo," I said. "We're doing your work. The work you've forced us to agree to do. If you are going to own us, you damn well better guide us."

Lu's hand tightened on my wrist, which was the only thing that stopped me from going off on an angry rant. I hated that we'd given up making our own choices, hated that our destiny was out of our hands.

Bo leaned back and rubbed his fingers down his goatee. "Own? I see it as I employ you, Brogan. Do you want out of our agreement? You bargained for that option. It's yours for the taking."

Go back to being just a spirit? Go back to never being able to touch Lu or be touched by her except for when the magic pocket watch ticked down the seconds?

Give up having more of a body, more of a voice, more of a life than I'd had in almost a hundred years?

My hand under Lu's fingers curled into a fist. "No," I said. "I don't want out of our agreement."

Bo searched my face and probably my thoughts. My skin went hot.

"This is a complication in my plans," he allowed. "You need to find the rabbit without me pointing to specifics. I think our needs still align."

And for a moment, the lights, the shadows, aged him, older than the stones.

"But nothing for me," Val grouched.

"Prove yourself useful." Bo leaned forward, shrugging off shadows, looking like Bo again. "Words to a god mean nothing. Faith means nothing. Actions and heart. That is the scale upon which a man is measured."

"What about a ghost?" Val asked.

Bo almost sighed, and I had to hide a smile. It was good to see I wasn't the only one who thought ghosts were the most annoying creatures drifting the earth.

"Ghosts are men. They're just dead men," Bo said.

The waitress swung by with two baskets of fried pickles and plonked them down on the table. "Need anything else?" she asked.

"This should do it," Bo said. "Thanks."

She turned and sauntered to the bar, already arguing that the favored contestant: "…couldn't survive a summer day in a mud puddle even if he were wearing water wings."

Bo popped a pickle in his mouth and chewed. He nodded toward the other pile of pickles and pointed at us.

I dragged it our way and tried one. Heat, salt, crunch and the tang of dill filled my mouth.

"Finding the rabbit will only be the beginning," he said. "Like I said, you'll have to choose how to follow through. I'm expecting you to do the right thing, and I won't tell you what that is. I'm not the god of destiny, not the god of fate. There are boundaries I'm already stepping on with this one."

"That doesn't sound ominous," Val complained.

"Boundaries with other gods?" Lu asked.

Bo wiped his fingers on a paper napkin, then wadded it up and scrubbed it over his mouth, scratching the bristles of his mustache. "Other ancients. Old promises, older mistakes. Any sign of that book yet?"

He said it casually, like it was nothing more than a basket of pickle chips. But there was an intensity in him, an edge of interest that was sharper than I'd seen before. He wanted that book. Wanted it more than he'd let on.

A chill washed down my back even though the bar was damp and muggy.

"We're still looking," I said.

"Nothing yet," Lu agreed.

He studied both of us, and I was reminded that making deals with gods was the folly of the desperate, the lost, and wayward fools like us.

"I told you I'd help you find it," he said all friendly-like, as if the intensity had never been there. "I'll do what I can. In the meantime, find the rabbit. Val will know it when he sees it, even if you don't.

"Don't let me down. Any of you." He rapped his knuckles on the table and stood. "We'll see each other soon, I'm sure. Safe travels."

He snagged up the basket and beer, and with a wave toward the waitress, who waved back absently, strode across the place, and out the door.

"That didn't sound like a threat at all, did it?" I asked Lu.

She rocked her hand in a maybe gesture and finally plucked up a pickle chip and bit through it.

"He wants the book," she said.

"I saw that."

"Not sure how I feel about it," she said.

"I feel suspicion and distrust. A whole lot of distrust."

"He said he'd help find it."

"Yep. But now I'm wondering why, if he wants it so bad, he won't just come out and say it."

"Gods," Lu said, as she went for another chip. "Always something up their sleeve. Who's the ghost?"

"I haven't asked. Name's Valentine, apparently."

"You could ask," Val said. "You could ask right now. I'm right here."

"Don't care," I muttered.

He growled, his wolf growled in agreement, then he just wasn't there anymore.

My shoulders dropped. I exhaled.

"He left?" Lu asked.

"That obvious?"

"For someone who knows you." She flashed me a little smile and pressed the toe of her shoe against the side of my shoe.

I didn't even wince.

"Where do you think we missed the rabbit?" I drank the last of the beer and rolled the bottle to study the label.

She shrugged. "We haven't gone far since we last saw Bo. Just across the rest of Illinois and about a hundred and fifty miles into Missouri. It won't be hard to backtrack."

"Backtrack all those miles looking for a tiny rabbit," I said. "It can't be a real rabbit, can it?"

Lu sipped the cherry cola, and I watched her eyes flutter shut as she savored the taste. I knew eating was more difficult for her now that she was a *thrawan*. All those years ago when she'd been attacked, she'd craved blood, but hadn't ever bitten anyone, worried that would force her into the final stage of vampirism.

She didn't crave blood now, or so she told me. She still needed food to stay alive, but ate very little of it. So when a cherry cola and damn fine pickle chips sparked her hunger, I was glad to see it.

"I don't think it's a real rabbit," she finally said. "But if not that, then what? A statue? A book? A metaphor?"

"I have no idea."

"He said we passed it."

"He didn't say we'd seen it, though. Gods have a way of keeping details up their sleeves, too."

She hummed in agreement, then ate another pickle chip. "Talk about the ghost."

"Youngish. Male. Maybe thirties? Pushy. Entitled. Wasn't about to take 'no' from a god, so he has guts, if not brains. Apparently murdered and looking for revenge."

"So: trouble."

"Aren't they all?"

"Oh, I don't know," she said with a wink. "Some spirits aren't too awful to have around."

"Hey, now. I take issue with that. I was never a ghost."

"Someone's splitting hairs."

"Someone wasn't even on the same spiritual plane as ghosts. You know that."

"I do know that," she said. "But I like the look of you all bothered and grumpy."

I opened my mouth to tell her I was not grumpy, realized how childish it sounded, and had the good sense to change my tack. I tugged her toward me. "How about I show you how bothered you make me?"

Her eyes were wide and not nearly as innocent as she thought. "Me?"

I grinned, then planted a kiss on her soft, smiling mouth. It was just a brief connection, but everything, everything I'd missed all these years.

"You taste like cherry soda," I said, my forehead resting against hers.

"You taste like home," she replied.

The voices at the bar rose and fell, and I just rested there, breathing, breathing.

"We don't have to do what Bo tells us to do," she said.

"Pretty sure we promised him we would."

"We have free will."

"Do we?"

"Of course we do. He can't take that away from us. We can choose to look for the rabbit later. Take our time. He didn't give us a time limit. We have the free will to choose our path forward, Brogan."

Her tone was hopeful and exasperated. She wanted me to believe her. Wanted me to believe free will was enough against the gods.

"All right," I said, even though she rolled her eyes at me. "We've got free will. If you think it's smart to take our time looking for the rabbit, then I'm on for that."

She rocked her face back and kissed me, quick, brief. "I think we get to make our own choices, and the gods can't change that."

I didn't want to argue, but I didn't see it the same way. "We made our choice. We chose to help him. In return for this." I touched the side of her face.

"Hooray, free will," she said.

I smiled. "Hooray."

She stood. "Let's hit the road. We have a lot of daylight hours left before we decide where we're staying tonight."

I grabbed up the last of the pickle chips and stuffed them in my mouth. "A motel."

"You didn't win our bet." She dropped bills on the table and started toward the door.

I was right behind her. "And you did?" The early afternoon was hot, and sweat quickly gathered across my neck and between my shoulder blades. Leaves rustled in the humid breeze, and I could just make out the sound of the Big Piney rushing along under the bridge.

Lu fished her sunglasses out of her pocket and put them on, her boots crunching across the gravel as she made her way to the truck.

"I bought something at the thrift shop that's worth selling. What did you buy, Brogan?"

"Postcards and clothes. Because you told me to."

"You had time to look around. I saw you eyeing that bookmark."

"Which I would have bought if Abbi hadn't shown up."

"I know." She flashed me a toothy smile. "Which is why I bought it. I'm gonna get a hundred bucks for that thing."

"It's magic," I said.

"I know."

"Headwaters?"

"Nope. I didn't offer it up to him."

"Then who's the sucker paying a hundred bucks for

a bookmark that probably only has residual—also probably useless—magic in it?"

"Crossroads."

I couldn't help it. I scowled.

"Come on, Brogan. You know she's a good person."

"I surely the shit do not know that."

"All right." She stopped in front of the truck, her hand on the door latch. "You know she's a knowledge-able person."

"Yes." It was all she was going to get. I didn't hate the woman. I didn't much like her either.

"She'll do the right thing with the magic. Lock it up if it's dangerous," Lu said.

"We both know it's not dangerous. It's a bookmark."

"Dangerous things come in small packages too."

"Sure. Obviously." What I couldn't figure out was why she hadn't tried to sell it to Headwaters.

"Maybe you just want to check in with her," I said, rounding the front of the truck to the passenger side. I opened the door and shouldered into the cab.

Lorde panted and made happy sounds, ready for the road again.

"Who?" Lu asked, getting in the driver's seat.

"Crossroads."

She pushed the key into the ignition, but instead of starting the engine, she twisted to look at me. "You don't like her."

"I didn't say that."

"Yes, you did."

That was one of the drawbacks of having only minutes at a time to see and speak to each other over nearly a hundred years: We each had gotten good—really good—at reading all the subtle, unspoken cues in the other.

"All right. I'm not fond."

She blinked. "You're not jealous of her are you?"

"No!" Too quick. Too loud.

Lorde barked once so I reached over and shushed her, petting her soft ears. "I'm not. It's just you've spent a lot of time with her over the years. And I've wanted to be the one you've spent that time with."

I was an idiot to admit it, and as soon as it was out of my mouth I felt small and petty.

Lu shifted in her seat, pulling one knee up so she could span the distance and reach me over the top of our furry dog. She tugged on my collar, pulling me close.

"I love you, Brogan Gauge. Forever."

I swallowed, and my heart stopped thumping so hard. I needed those words from her. Even after all these years.

"I love you too, Lula Gauge. Forever."

Lorde woofed, softer now, and I leaned toward Lu, accepting the kiss she offered.

"Good," Lu said. "Because you are stuck with me."

She released me and started the engine.

"Cupid rides a motorcycle?" Val said from the small space behind the seat. "Why would a god even need real transportation?"

I sighed. "Do we look like experts on gods to you?"

Lu glanced at me. "Val?"

"Unfortunately."

"Ask him where the rabbit is."

"I have no idea," he said. "But apparently I'll know it when I see it. You're welcome."

"He's useless," I said.

"Hey!"

"So far," Lu said.

"Better. She's a lot nicer than you."

Lorde shifted around and started sniffing the back of the seat. The ghost's wolf lifted its head, instantly interested. The two of them sniffed each other, ears twitching. Then Lorde sneezed and turned back around, tail wagging. She rested her big furry head on my thigh.

The wolf just tipped its head, then settled so close to Val, it was nearly inside him. I'd never seen a ghost with a wolf and would have asked him about it, but I really didn't want to get friendly with the guy.

The last thing we needed was a repeat haunting following us around.

"He thinks you're the nice one," I told Lu.

She just chuckled and headed back to the road. "Just wait until he gets to know me."

CHAPTER FIVE

The gas needle was sliding toward E, but Lu hadn't found a place she wanted to stop yet. Seeing Cupid had triggered something in her, and she was driving nice and slow, like she was trying to blend in with the rest of the world.

Or like she was looking for some safe place to hide for a while until the attention of the god was good and gone.

I knew the feeling. I wanted to take Lu somewhere safe and deal with this rabbit stuff on my own. Deal with this book stuff on my own, too, so I wouldn't have to worry about her getting hurt.

But one look at the stubborn set of her jaw, and I knew she'd never let me set her aside like that, not even if I did everything to convince her of my good intent.

"Could be a monument," I said. "Some sort of natural formation. A rock. A cave."

"Maybe," she said. "You can search for 'rabbit' on my phone. See if something turns up."

"I don't like that thing."

"You should get used to it."

"Why would I do that?"

She squinted and went silent.

We'd started our backtracking and were headed roughly northeast, just out of Doolittle. If the rabbit Bo wanted us to find was an actual rabbit, I hoped it would hop up alongside the road where we could spot it.

"This world, the living world, has changed," she said, "since you were in it."

I grunted.

She waited a while longer. I picked at the weather-stripping on the window.

"Technology, like a cell phone, is an important way to navigate the world now. Vital. Just like learning to drive—"

"I know how to drive," I interrupted.

She inhaled and waited, shifting how she was gripping the wheel. "Yes. Knowing how to drive is impor-tant to navigating the world. Especially how we live, you and I. On the Route."

My hands were in fists now, the dirt from the weath-erstripping stuck under my nails, making them ache.

Lorde sensed my discomfort and tapped her fuzzy tail.

It took a second, two, then I unclenched my hands and buried my fingers in her soft fur, petting her gently.

"Okay," I finally said, voice dry. I swallowed and tried again, this time tossing a smile her way. "Give me that devil's box and talk me through it."

"I can do it," Valentine said. "I know how to use a phone."

"I don't need your opinion," I groused.

"Me or Val?" Lu handed me her phone.

"Val. Your opinion I'll always want."

"Good. Then I have some things to say about your cooking."

"Nope," I interrupted. "My cooking is five stars. Let's focus on the hand computer."

"Phone. It's a phone, Brogan."

"It's mostly not." I bent to study the screen and poked at it. Nothing happened.

"You turn it on here," Val said, his ghostly arm coming down from behind me to wave in front of my face.

"I can see where it turns on, Val. Stop. Look. How old were you when you died?"

He pulled his arm back. "Thirty-two. Why?"

"What year was it?"

"Last year."

"So you've only been dead a year. That makes you either thirty-three or a one-year-old. My bet's on the latter."

"What are you saying? What's that supposed to mean?"

"It means you are a child, and I don't need your help."

"Oh, fuck off," Val said. "You're older than dirt. Click on one of the squares."

I grinned at his exasperated tone. "Which one of the squares?"

"Icons," Lu said.

"Icons," I repeated. "Which one lets me search the thing?"

"The internet," Val said. "You're searching the internet."

"I know it's called the internet. I've been mostly dead, not deaf."

"Google," Lu said. "It looks like a G."

"All right. Let's see." I poked and swiped, muttered under my breath and snicked air through my teeth as I swiped again. "G. Got it. Press like a button. There it is. Think I should just type rabbit?"

"No," Lu said. "Too broad of a search term. Something more specific."

"Rabbit of the gods?"

"Brogan."

"Rabbits in Missouri? Rabbits on the Route? Famous Rabbits Cupid has a *thing* for?"

"Type in Missouri and landmark and rabbit."

"It's not doing anything."

"Tap the magnifying glass symbol."

I did so.

"There's a Kung Fu Rabbit in St. Louis. It's a statue. Earth Bunny in Webster Groves. Also a statue. Something called an Ecovillage and another statue. This one's two white bunnies, titled: Two Rabbits. Well, that's original."

"Ask Val if any of that is what we're looking for."

"I don't think any of those statues are what we're looking for," he said. "But I won't know until I see them, right?"

We were just outside Rolla now. We couldn't put off getting gas. Just ahead was a truck stop that advertised "Home Cookin' From Scratch Try The Gravy." It had a gravel lot, a carwash in the back, and a good grassy area for Lorde.

The whole place looked deserted.

Lu pulled off the road, down the dusty side street, and into the empty parking lot.

"Val says he'll know it when he sees it," I said. "Again, not a lot of help." I set the phone on the dash.

Lu pulled up to the pump.

"I'm plenty of help. If you listened to me, jackass." Val sniffed and stared out the side window.

"Good enough," Lu said. "Three sets of eyes are better than two. Do you mind taking Lorde for her walk?"

"I got it." I fished Lorde's leash out from under the seat, then levered my way out the door.

Being over-large and jammed into this tin can made exiting the cab feel like I was squeezing myself out of a toothpaste tube. The sun was a furnace just pumping out the heat. At least I'd had a chance to change into the jeans.

Lu watched me with a little smile on her face, then hopped easily out of the cab. She slid her fingers into her back pocket and dug out her slim wallet. She should probably put on a hat, but before I could suggest it, she was at the pump, taking the nozzle to the tank.

Lorde shook, and her tags jingled.

"All right," I said. "Let's stretch those legs." I clipped on her leash and stepped aside so she could jump down.

"You coming?" I asked Val.

His gaze came back from a distance and he frowned. His wolf was standing now, still staring into that distance. "No," he said. "I think… I think I'll stay here."

I turned an eye toward the sky, across the busy road where storm clouds built a reef of grays across the horizon. I didn't see anything out of the ordinary, but something in the air made my gut tighten.

Lorde whined and pulled on the leash. "Okay, girl, let's find you some grass."

I took her to the wide grassy area, glancing back at Lu every now and then.

Lorde, nose to the ground, seemed fascinated by the smells.

My gaze kept returning to the Route and the clouds beyond it.

Interstate 44 had been built right on top of the Route, so the traffic moved quickly here, but there was something strangely slow about everything else, as if the air were molasses thick and time had lost its tick. Maybe it was the brewing storm, the fall of barometric pressure messing with my senses.

Maybe it was just the age of the place—the squat concrete building covered by advertisements for beer, cigarettes, and energy drinks that hadn't been popular in years.

No. Something was off. Something was wrong.

The flicker of a shadow to my left pulled my gaze that way, but it winked out of my line of vision before I could catch it.

Lorde finally lifted her head and scented the air. She growled softly, then whined.

"Come, on, sweetheart." I tugged on her leash, itchy to move. "Let's go back to the truck."

The wind picked up suddenly, a push of heat and moisture carrying the stench of sunbaked concrete and gasoline fumes.

It shoved my hair away from my eyes, and a voice whispered: "*I taste magic.*"

Not a ghost. I knew ghosts. They didn't speak in this kind of fluting whisper.

The wind fell, drawing the heat away with it, and then whipped again.

"*Blood and thread. Strange, the key upon her skin.*"

The wind grew hotter, slashing at my exposed skin, face, neck, arms.

I couldn't move. My heart hammered like I was running, but my feet would not lift. Panic poured cold gasoline over my nerves but my body didn't fire.

Lorde tugged the leash taut, whining.

I yelled for Lu, and she turned…slowly, so slowly, like a dream. Like a nightmare.

A shock of cold smacked me hard in the chest. I stumbled backward, blinking as if I'd been asleep standing.

"Move!" Valentine's eyes flashed red, then he was running toward Lu.

Now I could see them. A howl, a stampede, a wailing charge of spectral creatures, nearly invisible to the eye, rushing across the parking lot, flying over the dirt and pavement like ribbons of smoke and teeth and claws on a hurricane wind.

Rushing toward Lu.

I ran.

Lorde snarled and barked. Ahead of us Val spooked out and instantly stood in front of Lu who had turned toward us, knife in her hand. She couldn't see the creatures coming like an avalanche, storming over the Route.

The ghost wolf lowered his head and bared his teeth. Val matched its stance facing down the creatures.

"Lu!" I yelled again, pointing north, just as the wave of creatures crested and began to crash downward over her.

Val and the wolf leaped up into the creatures, breaking the momentum of the wave. The creatures scattered and lurched skyward, a shrieking, grasping, clawing dust devil that faded and was gone just as suddenly as it had begun.

I was at Lu's side, pulling her into me, my hands and arms shaking. "Did they touch you? Did they hurt you?" The words were fear-thin, barely understandable, even to my own ears.

Blood arrowed across her neck. Only a scratch, only a scratch, but my fear snapped right on over into rage.

"No," Lu said. "Brogan, look at me. I'm fine. It's a scratch."

But the words I'd heard on the wind came back to me: *Blood and thread. Strange, the key upon her skin.*

"They marked you."

"Something did," she said. "It's okay, Brogan. I can take care of myself. I'm okay."

I finally unlocked my arms and let her step back enough I could inspect the mark. It *was* just a scratch and had already stopped bleeding.

"Did you hear them?" I asked. "Did you see them?"

"I didn't hear anything," she said, sheathing her knife, "except you yelling and Lorde barking."

The gas nozzle clunked, and I jumped. Lu turned and removed it from the tank, setting it back in its cradle.

"I know there were creatures on the wind," she said. "I felt fingers digging at the chain." She touched the chain on her neck, then leaned her hip into Silver and crossed her arms over her chest.

"When I pulled my knife, the fingers were gone. Now it's your turn. What happened? What did you see?"

Lorde moved over to her and snuffled around her feet and legs. Lu reached down and petted Lorde's head.

"There was something in the wind. Old magic."

"How old?" she asked.

My gaze darted to the thin, dry line of blood on her neck, then back to her honey eyes. "You didn't see any of them?"

"No."

"Ancient, I think. They came on the gust of wind across the Route, across the parking lot. Too much like smoke for me to make out details."

"Not ghosts?"

"No. They were dark. From somewhere Beneath." I

considered not telling her the next bit, but we didn't need lies between us. "Val pushed me, snapped me out of a…I don't know…hypnosis."

Her eyebrows rose. "Did he?"

"By then the creatures were almost on you, falling like a wave."

"And what did they say? You heard them."

"They said they tasted magic. Something about blood and thread and a strange key on her skin. I'm assuming your skin."

"All right," she said. "I like that you could hear them and see them. That's good. I'm fine, remember?"

"You're bleeding."

"For the last time, Brogan, I can take care of myself against one little wave of monsters." She pushed stray strands of hair off her forehead and looked away for a long moment before digging up a small smile.

"I'm not bleeding. Not anymore. You scared them off."

I scowled at the road and rubbed the back of my neck. "That wasn't me. That was Valentine too."

"Okay, so maybe having him around is a good thing. Another set of eyes, another skill set to help with this stuff. Keep us both safe."

"One good deed does not a soul measure."

"It was two." She chuckled. "I didn't think you could scowl harder."

I pointed at her. "Just because he does a couple of nice things doesn't change my opinion of him. If we leave now, maybe he'll stay behind."

"He wants to be your friend."

"You don't know that. You can't hear him."

"I do know that. Because everyone wants to be your friend."

I opened my mouth, then closed it.

"Whatever that attack was, whatever those creatures were," she said, "he helped us. Both of us. Plus, he's going to help us find the rabbit, so let's not ditch him yet, okay?"

"Those creatures were old magic," I said. "Maybe even the Hush. Lots of caverns and caves in these hills."

She pushed off the truck and tugged on my hips, bringing me close. "Hush from the legends? No one has seen them in hundreds of years."

I ran one finger down the links of the chain on the unscratched side of her throat. "Things come back, get stirred up. Might be Hush. Might be some other old magic."

My finger slipped under the chain and followed it beneath the collar of her shirt. She shivered from my touch. I tried not to ask her if she was okay again, tried just to trust that she would tell me if she wasn't.

"What about Val?" she asked.

"What about him?"

"He shoved you. For a good reason. It isn't easy for a ghost to manifest physically."

I grunted. "He gets a pass this time."

She tucked her hands in my back pockets. "You like him."

"I do not. But he helped you. Helped us."

"You should thank him."

"He's not here."

"Love the jeans," she said.

I smiled, and knew it was wolfish. "You loved me stripping beside the road to put them on even better."

"I do enjoy a free show." She squeezed my ass, then stepped back. "Wanna drive?"

"All right."

"You don't have to." She bent to scrub at Lorde's ears. "Want some water, sweet girl?"

Lorde wagged her tail, and I handed Lu her leash. "I'll get her bowl. And I'm driving."

I walked around the back of Silver, my eyes searching that horizon and those clouds. Lorde made happy little half-howling sounds while Lu cooed at her.

When I was out of Lu's line of sight, I fully exhaled, letting the fear and adrenalin shake through me. I'd seen my share of monsters on the road.

But these spirits, whatever they had been, were malevolent. Violent. More than that, they were hungry.

Whether they were hungry for the magic Lu carried around her neck, or the magic that had changed her from human to something else, I didn't know.

But I had been frozen, absolutely stuck, and unable to do anything to save her. She could have been killed while I just stood there and watched.

I shuddered, mopped the wet heat of the day off my face, and shuddered again feeling sick.

I dried my palm on my pants and dug for Lorde's water bowl.

When I returned to Lu, I smiled and told her again that I was fine.

I didn't know if she believed me. I could feel her gaze on me as I excused myself to use the bathroom.

And if I stood there, staring at my blurry reflection in the scratched metal mirror for too long, shivering while tepid water ran over my fingers, well, I was the only one to know.

CHAPTER SIX

I liked driving. Always had in the short time I'd been alive. But the vehicles from back in my day were bundles of twine and rubber compared to modern cars.

And this truck, Silver, was a beast.

"Gas pedal, Brogan. Give it a push. You're not gonna get anything in life pussyfooting around."

"I know the speed limit."

"It's not twenty-five."

"I'm going forty-five." I glanced at the speedometer, which was, thankfully, an actual dial with a hand showing my speed. "Forty-one. Close enough."

Lu slouched in the passenger side of the seat, her back braced against the door, one knee up against the back of the seat, one foot on the floor, Lorde half draped across her lap. She straightened her leg, her bare foot digging at my butt.

"Never thought I'd have to tell a woman to keep her feet off my ass," I said. "Hands, maybe."

An eighteen-wheeler crept up on us, and I was thinking I should slow down even more so it would pass.

"I like your ass," she said lazily. Her toes slipped between my butt and the seat, and she managed to wiggle them a little.

That got me looking over at her, but just a quick glance. "How about you like it when I'm not driving this thing?"

"Relax," she said, with a toe wiggle. "You're doing just fine. Is it hot in here?" She plucked at her tank top, lifting it away just enough that I could see the edge of her lace bra and a lot of pale, soft skin. "It feels hot in here."

"Keep that up, and I won't be the one to blame for crashing this thing."

She wiggled her toes again, chuckling, then closed her eyes and dropped her hand on Lorde's head. "I trust you," she said. "You are a man of intense focus and great reflexes. Don't worry about the big rig following you. It's gonna pass. Breathe. Relax. Let the road spool on by."

She wasn't even sitting at an angle that would allow her to see what was behind us, but she knew me well enough to know what I was tensed up about.

I took a deeper breath and tried to relax my grip on the wheel, leaning back into the seat instead of hunching forward.

The big rig sped up and passed me in the left lane.

"You were right," I said. Lu just hummed, not even stirring. She felt safe enough to fall asleep while I was driving and it did a lot of good for my confidence.

"I know you don't like me," Val said from some-where behind me to my left. "But whatever that was back there at the gas station, it wanted the necklace she's wearing."

I thought about that for a minute, chewing on how much I should share with him.

Ghosts, in my experience, were attention-seeking troublemakers. Once they'd found a way to get a living person to notice them, they were impossible to get rid of.

But Val had stepped up when it mattered most. When I'd been frozen.

"They want the magic in it, maybe," I said, hoping my voice was quiet enough not to wake Lu.

Val made a considering noise. "It's a key, isn't it?"

"The pocket watch?"

"The silver feather."

The feather was the key to a book of magic Lu had nearly taken a bullet for, and which our stupidly brave dog had taken instead when she put herself in the line of fire.

A hunter—a human who hunted monsters—had stolen the book from us, even though we'd gone to a lot of trouble to retrieve it from a ghost.

"The key's powerful," Val said, fishing for details.

"It is," I agreed.

He puffed out a frustrated breath. "I think the rabbit is more than a statue or a building or a point on the map. I think it's alive."

"A real rabbit?"

"No. And maybe not human. Probably not human. But alive."

"Well, if you see it, tell me. The sooner we find it, the sooner you can go home."

"I'm dead. I don't have a home."

I shouldn't get suckered in by the bitterness in his voice. But I'd been there, drifting alongside the living and feeling more lost than found. I still woke in the middle of the night expecting Lu to no longer be able to feel my touch, hear my voice.

"You were born somewhere," I said. "Spent your life somewhere. Near the bar?"

"Devil's Elbow? No. Up the road a ways, though. Mostly." He fell silent and I wondered how many of his memories were still fresh. Wondered if life—the people he loved, hated, the places he'd called his own—were fading while his time as something apart from the world grew richer.

I didn't ask him about family, wasn't sure he wanted to be reminded of what he'd lost. He didn't say anything else, but from what I could see of him in the rearview mirror, he was staring at some middle distance, his wolf lying with its head on his lap.

Everyone was cozy, so I left the radio off, settled my shoulders to ease the hitch in my neck, and drove east.

The road rolled by, slow and steady, the horizon never growing closer. Even though I was driving instead of riding invisible in the passenger seat, this was familiar, and in its way, comforting.

I knew the dangers on the road, or at least most of them. But I wanted miles between those creatures who had marked Lu before we stopped for the night, no matter what Cupid wanted.

"Stop over there."

We were pulling into St. Clair, the Big Hunt Thrift and Junk just ahead.

"We've been there already," I said.

"Go there again. Go there now."

"Do you think the rabbit's in there? We looked."

"Pull over."

I was not going to take orders from a ghost.

"Please," he added.

I eased off of the gas and guided the truck into the parking lot. The shop was closed. There were no other cars.

"You going to ghost your way in there?" I asked. But when I glanced in the rearview, Val was gone.

"Is he?" Lu sat, and Lorde yawned, her black tongue curling as she tried to stretch in the small space.

"I don't know. I'll go—no, I think he's that way." I pointed toward the edge of the parking lot, to the grass and trees.

"Let's see." Lu touched my arm. Then she was out the door, Lorde right on her heels.

I got out of the truck, stiff from both sitting and the attention and focus it took to drive, unused to those normal things.

Lu's head tipped up, as if she could smell a storm on the wind, and I took a sniff. There might be a storm coming but it hadn't hit yet. Lorde happily nosed her way to the grass so she could pee.

Lu waited for me to come up beside her, then dropped her hand, waiting for me to find it with my own.

The moment our fingers touched I felt grounded, settled. Home.

I wondered if this was the thing Val was missing. A home didn't have to be a place. It could be a person, or a part of you that you couldn't exist without. A part of you that you would fight to keep hold of, no matter the consequences.

Lu squeezed my fingers lightly, then started walking. "This way?"

I angled us a bit to the left. "He's staring at the trees, and that wolf of his is pacing in front of him."

"He has a wolf?"

"Uh…I didn't say that before?"

"No, Brogan, you didn't. A ghost wolf?"

"I suppose."

"Why…" Then her eyes narrowed. "Is Val a were-wolf? A shape shifter?"

"I've never heard of a werewolf ghost. Can that even exist?"

The look she gave me was a reminder that I wasn't something people thought could even exist.

"Fine, just because I haven't heard of it," I allowed.

"Val," Lu said, "are you a werewolf? A shifter?"

"He was," another voice said.

The man who pulled away from the shadow of the tree had been so hidden, even Lorde hadn't detected him.

He was one of Summer's guards, the one with ice-chipped eyes, who'd been kind to the girl, Abbi.

"You knew Valentine?" Lu asked.

"Is he here?" he asked in lieu of an answer. "I thought I felt his hate."

I took a better look at the ghost. Val's fists were clenched, his wolf crouched, ready to leap, rend, kill. The man's and wolf's eyes glowed red, their ghostly forms outlined in a silver so bright, it burned black.

Val did not like this guy. "You're Danube, right?" I asked, in case I'd need to deal with a possession or a killing.

"Yes. I'm his brother."

I didn't see the similarity, other than that they both had dark hair and there was something of the wolf about them.

Val snarled. "Brother, my ass. In name maybe. Never in blood."

"Val doesn't agree," I noted.

Danube's eyes widened and he looked away from us to scan the area in front of him. "You can see him? He's here? You can hear him?"

Before I could answer, Val and his wolf bolted forward. Between one stride and the next, the man and wolf blended into one spirit, more wolf than man, a silver ghost made of fang, claws, and fury.

He was running straight at Danube.

"Shit." I ran after him.

It was a knee-jerk reaction. I didn't even think. I just acted, not remembering I was no longer in spirit form, but was a man of bone and blood and muscle.

I couldn't instantly transport myself anywhere like I used to. Which meant I was nowhere near close enough to grab Val. I'd have to stop him another way.

Those thoughts rapid fired through my brain.

And then…

I reached out with my hands, knowing what it felt like to grab a ghost, knowing the shock of connecting to a level of existence not in line with my own.

It hadn't been easy to catch a ghost when I'd been a spirit.

It wasn't easier now.

I shouted as pain licked fire in my muscles, cramping my calves, my stomach, my arms as if I'd been dipped into a vat of burning coals.

My empty hands shook, and then I felt the edges of Valentine's spirit, my fingers sliding into ice, plunging into an electric cold.

I yanked.

Val was suddenly absolutely still, suspended inches away from Danube's face.

My hands froze and burned as I struggled to hold the fleeting essence of the man.

Danube took a step back, then another. "He's here. He's right here. Isn't he?"

Lu strode up next to me, and I was shocked to find I'd only taken three steps. It felt like I'd been running on lightning, my breathing coming hard and fast.

"Val," Lu said. "You need to back away from Danube. If you do, Brogan will let you go."

I blinked the sting of sweat out of my eyes but didn't dare move, didn't dare speak. I didn't know exactly how I had grabbed the ghost much less how I was holding him frozen. But however I had done it, it was damned exhausting.

If Val didn't do what Lu said real quick like, I wasn't going to be able to hold him anyway.

Even though Val didn't move, my hold on him changed, as if he had stopped running, stopped pushing. The shape of him changed too, sliding away from wolf and more toward man.

"Do we have an understanding?" Lu asked.

I eased my hold, just slightly.

"Yes," he growled.

I released him. He and his wolf separated, his wolf stepping forward, head down, facing Danube. Val didn't make any moves, although the lines of his body were hatred and anger.

Sweat stuck the T-shirt to my back, prickling as it crawled down from my pits. I lifted one arm and swiped the cotton over my face. "Keep your word, and we won't have any problems," I said.

"Why are you here?" Lu asked.

"I drove with you," Valentine answered.

"She's not talking to you," I said. "You," I said to the werewolf, who had backed off several strides, but still hadn't smartened up enough to run.

"I heard you coming." He narrowed his eyes, looking for Val and not finding him. "Not a lot of people drive a truck that old."

I resisted the urge to poke fun at Lu, as I'd been against the truck from the start.

"Why does it matter to you if we're here?" I asked.

"I think you're looking for something."

Lu and I waited. Val quietly snarled.

"Abbi liked you."

I crossed my arms to keep from scrubbing at the itch between my shoulder blades. The air was thick, not a breath of wind. It felt like we hung there, suspended. Like we'd all dived down deep to get to this place and were treading water.

"She trusts too easily. She doesn't like everyone, believe it or not. But she's young," he said, though it didn't sound like he was convinced that that was wholly true. "Sometimes." A wry smile hit his face, and it transformed him from a menacing figure, to something a little more human.

"She asked us for a ride. To find something for her," Lu said.

Just like that, the smile was gone. "We're handling that. You should go. Before Summer finds you sniffing around here."

"Why? Does she have something to hide?" I asked.

Val snarled again, his fists clenched. "Tell him he was wrong." He winked out of existence and was standing next to me, cold fury. "Tell him he was wrong about the Shadow."

"What shadow?" I asked.

"Shadow?" Danube asked. "Is that what you're here for?"

I had no idea what either of them were talking about, and since Lu could only hear half of the conversation, she was as in the dark as me.

"Abbi talked about a shadow," Lu said. "A shadow in the dark."

And didn't that sound ominous when she said it that way?

Danube walked toward us, and Val tensed. I put out a hand to stop Val from lunging at the guy again. To my surprise, he obeyed.

"Tell him he was wrong about the Shadow."

I still didn't take orders from ghosts, but my gut told me this was tied up with more than Val's anger. Tied up with more than Val's death. Somehow Abbi was involved, and I would never stand aside when a child might be in danger.

"Val says you were wrong about the shadow."

The man froze. What color he'd had in his face, what anger, drained away fast, leaving him pale, eyes wide in shock. Or fear.

"Val?" he breathed. "Is he. Can you talk to him?"

"Tell him it's not lost. It's trapped. Tell him I did the job he asked me to do, and he owes me. He *owes* me."

"What shadow are we talking about?" Lu asked.

"That isn't for you to know," Danube said, like he could just shove all the worms back into the can without getting his fingers dirty. "Is Val here?"

"Tell him," Val said again. "I'm here. I did his job. He owes me."

I glanced at Lu. She didn't seem worried, but then, it would take more than a strange conversation with a werewolf and ghost to get her riled. Lorde stood at her side, tense as she stared at Danube. Her ears and tail were up, like she was in high alert, but not ready to attack. Not yet.

"Val's here."

Danube swallowed and nodded, his hand rising

slightly. "Can I… Can you tell me where… Tell him I'm sorry. I couldn't get to him in time. I tried."

"He ran. I know he ran," Val said. "I heard him."

"Brogan?" Lu asked.

"Yeah, it's not clear to me either," I said. "Val said Danube was wrong about the shadow. Said it's not lost. It's trapped. That mean something to you?"

I didn't think the man could look any more ashen, but he did. "Did he…" Danube pulled his hand to the back of his neck. "He didn't try to…Holy Luna, tell me he didn't try to free it."

"Of course I did!" Val yelled. "He told me if I found it, he'd let me in. I'd be a part of them, I'd be his brother, I would *belong*. But instead, he let them just throw me away like garbage. Like I'm *nothing*.

"Fuck it. It doesn't matter. Tell him he owes me."

"I don't know what you promised Val," I said, "but he says you owe him. And I say you owe us an explanation. What is the shadow? Why is everyone looking for it? Why did it get Val killed? And what does this have to do with Abbi?"

I thought Danube would break, that he'd tell us enough for all of this to make sense. But instead he shored up like concrete setting under the blazing sun. His chin lifted, his shoulders drew back.

"I do owe you, Val. I haven't forgotten. I'll find a way, to… I don't know what I can do, but I'll find a way to do right by you. I was wrong. Stupid to let you go." Danube swallowed. "I owe you."

"Fuck," Val breathed, and there was anger, but more, there was sorrow and pain.

"We're looking for a rabbit," Lu said. "Does Abbi have something to do with a rabbit? A magical rabbit?"

"Don't," he said. "Abbi is none of your concern. She can't be. But she is safe in our hands, safe in our territory. She's chosen to be with us, you saw that. But if you want to stay alive," his gaze flicked to both of us, and his nostrils flared, as if he could smell the monsters we were, "stay out of the dark, stay out of the caves, and stay away from shadows."

He searched the middle distance, looking, I assumed, for Val.

"I haven't forgotten you, brother. I haven't abandoned you. Not then. Not now."

Val choked, one harsh sob shaking his head, eyes screwed shut. His wolf paced a circle around the ghost's feet, then stood in front of him, lifting up to put huge paws on his shoulders. Val's arms wrapped around the wolf, then the ghost disappeared.

I wiped more sweat off my face. "He's gone."

Danube nodded, and nodded, then he turned. "Don't return," he said over his shoulder.

Within one step, he was no longer a man, but a rangy grey and brown wolf with a lighter spot on his chest and one foot. The wolf did not look back but ran, silent and swift, into the long grasses and evening shadows.

"I don't think any of that was helpful," I noted. All of it hit me at once. My knees turned to room-temperature butter, and I decided it might be time to take a nice rest in the dirt and gravel.

Lu moved to hook her arm through mine. "Can you make it to the truck?"

"Of course I can make it to the truck. I'm fine."

"I know," she said.

"I just need some water. It's hot. Why is it always so hot?" It was more than my knees now. My head was starting to drift and wobble, like a balloon bouncing on a string.

"Because we're in Missouri."

"Well, you'd think they'd invest in some shade around here."

"Almost there," she said.

I saved the rest of my breath for breathing, which turned out to be a wise decision. It took all I had in me to mount up into the passenger side of the cab. It wasn't the heat that had wrung all the energy out of me. Fighting with the ghost, forcing him to stop, forcing him to do what I wanted him to do had me thinking passing out might be in my very near future.

I didn't remember Lu shutting the door, didn't remember her and Lorde getting in on the other side, but when she started the truck, I tried to open my eyes.

"It's okay," she said. "I'm going to find us a place to sleep. Just rest."

And honestly, rest was all I could do.

CHAPTER SEVEN

The cup pressed against my lips was cool, and I woke to the very real need to drink as much of the water as I could.

Lu leaned in the open door of the truck, one hand on my thigh, the other holding the cup to my lips. "Just a few sips. I don't want you sick."

I took the cup from her and gulped. She tried to take it from me, but I caught her hand with my free hand and finished the water.

"Stubborn," she said. "I see only filling the cup halfway was a good choice on my part."

"Is there any more?"

"Yes, but not yet. How are you feeling?"

I rubbed at my eye with a knuckle and only then realized it was dark out, evening long gone while I'd slept. The bugs and other critters of the night had found their voices and were giving it all they had.

I thought we couldn't be that far from the road, but

we must at least be in a field or hollow, as there were no sounds of traffic.

"Good," I said. "I don't know how or why that knocked me out."

"Brogan, you reached between the veils of reality and contained a vengeful spirit."

"And?"

She huffed and squeezed my thigh. "It's a lot. I only know a few people who can do that, and they use magic."

"Maybe I used magic."

"No, you just—" She shook her head. "You just used you. Your will."

"Not that it did much good. Both of those were-wolves have secrets," I said. "And they talk in circles." I wiggled the cup. "Can we give more water a try?"

"Come get in the back."

She stepped back, and the movement of her was like a dance I was helpless to resist. Where Lula Gauge walked, so, too, would I, step in step.

So I hauled my legs around and out the door and stood on the grass. I was tired, sure, but no longer exhausted. I followed Lu to the back of the truck.

She'd unpacked the mattress, pillows, sleeping bags, and the handmade quilt she'd picked up at the yard sale back in the little town of Cuba.

"I thought we were headed to a hotel," I said. "Hot shower? Room service?"

"Nope. I won the bet. I found the magic bookmark."

"Beg to differ."

"All right. I picked up the magic bookmark. You

didn't even touch it."

"I would have if Abbi hadn't interrupted us."

Lu hopped up into the truck bed. Lorde lifted her head, the tags on her collar jangling as she moved out of the way for us. I crawled up onto our bed and had to admit that a hotel bed would not have been any softer or more welcome than this.

I stretched out on my stomach, herding a pillow down to me and sighing in deep contentment.

Lu settled next to me, her hand resting on my neck, working the muscles there before stroking down my spine. "Feel better?"

"Well, it's not a hot shower—" I began, then yelped as Lu pinched my side. I grinned.

"We can shower at a truck stop tomorrow. Tonight… Tonight, I need this," she said.

I shifted around, shoving the pillow under my head as I flipped, then lay on my side facing her.

"You could have died, Brogan."

This was news to me. "When?"

"When you grabbed hold of the ghost. When you argued with a werewolf."

"Ah. That. You were there."

Even in the darkness, I could see her sunlight eyes watching me. "What does that mean?"

"You were there. So I wasn't worried about dying."

Her eyes closed for a moment too long, and she tipped her face to the sky. "I need you to be more care-ful. Need you to… Not do that kind of thing."

I just hummed and tugged on the edge of her shirt.

She resisted a second or two, then scooted down and

curled into my body, her head tucking beneath my chin. I wrapped my arms around her.

"Do you want the rest of the water?"

I did. I really did, but having her in my arms and knowing I could hold her like this for as long as I wanted was more important.

"Later." I closed my eyes, felt myself drifting off, and opened them again.

The stars spun out above me like a diamond-beaded net cast across a dark sea. It was beautiful, the sky. The moon had waned to a sliver of a crescent that cast almost no light, making the darkness darker, while starlight caught like distant fire.

It was Lu's fingers, though, gently tracing my arm, her body so close and warm against me, that was the real treasure.

"I love you, Brogan Gauge," she said, as she always had.

"I love you too, Lula Gauge," I replied, as I always would.

I thought I wouldn't be able to sleep. But with Lu in my arms, and Lorde at my feet, and a soft breeze finally, finally wicking the heat from the ground, from the trees, and from me, I fell down and down, over and out.

"R*un.*" The deep voice was a cat-like growl, frantic. Thick fingers crawled across my lips, dug into my cheeks, pressed into the skin of my forehead, bruising bone. "*The moon, the moon. You must save the moon.*"

Those fingers lifted, scrabbling through my hair and

pulling until the roots stung.

"*Find her…*"

I took a huge breath and opened my eyes, disoriented in the suffocating darkness.

There were no stars above me, no mattress beneath me, and no Lu in my arms.

Everything was stone: beneath, around, above. Even the air tasted of stone, as if I inhaled a hillside, slick minerals, and earthen mold.

A cave? A dream?

Or something else altogether? Some kind of magic.

Voices came from the walls, from the ground, from the ceiling above. They were stone, darkness, but they were more than that.

These voices were old. Something evil. Something hungry.

"*Lost soul. We see you.*"

The shadows thickened, darkness in all the shades of insanity oozing around me, dripping into my ears, my eyes, my lungs. I struggled to sit.

"*Soul-torn wanderer. We have seen you. Bleeding your sorrow.*" The voices drew closer, pulling out of stone, squeezing through the pores, the cracks, the shattered, spreading into the breath of this place.

I pressed my palm upon the ground, cold and sharp, the sting of razors cutting my skin. I staggered to my feet, squaring toward the voices that seemed to come from everywhere.

"You may see me," I said, blinking hard and scanning the darkness, "but I cannot see you. Show yourself."

The air was cold, cold, cold. If I could see, my breath would be a frozen cloud. Frost crawled across my skin, ice gathered in the folds of my clothing.

"*Hush, hush,*" a thousand voices whispered from around me, a scrabble of nightmares, a chorus of horror. "*Wayward soul. Hush, hush, hush. Mother comes. Mother Hush. Hush, hush.*"

There was no light, but my eyes were adjusting. Just enough to make out jagged edges, stone.

And then there was a new voice.

"*Here now, broken marrow.*" The voice was solid, the strike of a hammer on the roots of an ancient tree, the shriek of claws scaling obsidian cliffs. "*I am here.*"

All other sounds extinguished, and the cavern filled with eerie light.

Mother Hush appeared.

She was tall, taller than me—

—*a tatter of bones, a ruffle of wings, spider silk for skin, and starlight eyes*—

—tall enough she should have had to stoop in this small cavern. But the shadows were a part of her, shifting and parting so she could have space among them.

The queen, the creature, the…

…*Mother Hush…*

…Mother Hush wore leaves and slices of stone and agate that clattered and shushed in flowing layers. Lacy, luminescent lichen drew delicate, glowing edges around her, illuminating her face.

She was—

—*terrifying*—

—beautiful and horrifying in a way that hit my gut and made the hair on my body rise.

Her eyes were wide black orbs. Her too-small mouth and blackened lips curved in a sharp, pointed jaw. The entirety of her face was hard, angled, and too long.

White hair floated away from her skull, and when she lifted her hands, one had too many fingers, spider-like, the other too few.

She was vaguely fae, vaguely insect, wholly unfettered magic of the old worlds beneath.

"Hush," I whispered, and all the voices in the dark moaned.

"*You know my kind, ragged bones?*"

"Only stories. The wise steer wide of you and grant you peace."

Her expression shifted, like smoke curling at a wick, intrigued. "*Are you a wise man, BroGan Gaayge?*"

I shuddered at my name falling frozen from her mouth.

"I would give you peace," I said in answer.

She shifted, drifting closer to me with a soft clatter.

"*So few wise men in the worlds, above or beneath.*" Her hand with too many fingers rose, one finger hooked toward me, the others writhing like snakes. "*Even fewer wise gods. Yes?*"

I knew better than to agree with any creature who had the power to bind with words. The Hush or at least this very powerful Hush, most definitely had that power.

The tales said the Hush were a blight upon the land long gone. Eradicated when technology devoured the wild spaces.

But there were still pockets of wild in the world, even here, along the Route.

Perhaps the Hush were reclaiming old passageways, spaces they had lived in before man invented machines.

"*No?*" she asked. "*You will not speak? Perhaps you are a little wise, BroGan Gaayge. If you wish to live...*" All her fingers stilled.

My arms suddenly jerked back, my legs caught in shackles that grew from stone and iron. A vice clamped around my neck and squeezed, reducing me to shallow sips of stagnant air.

"Do not struggle," a low, male voice said near my ear. "I will keep you safe." He stood close to me, very close, though I could not see him. He shifted and the vice—his hand—around my neck eased slightly.

"*If you wish to live,*" Mother Hush sang, advancing with the click of claws on stone. "*I will have one thing from you.*"

"You cannot bind me," I whispered.

"*Because a god favors you?*" She opened her mouth and showed me too many rows of teeth. "*I see who binds you and he is nothing to you. His ties are nothing. He is nothing.*

"*But there is more. A soul binds you. Love binds you. That will be your noose.*"

I struggled, but the creature holding me growled, his winter's breath freezing in the air.

"Be still," he whispered, "and you may live."

I stilled, and the shackles on my ankles and arms relaxed a fraction.

"*You have the key,*" Mother Hush cooed. "*You will find*

the binding, our Strange weave, and return what was stolen from us."

None of it made sense, but the words burned into me as if they were written in lightning across my eyes.

"The book. Ours. The Strange weave binding. Ours. We would have it." Her needle sharp fingers reached for me, thin spider-silk webbing dripped from the sharp tip of each finger.

I jerked my head back and lunged against my bindings, but could not move.

"Hush," she sang. Fast as a wing, her finger drew across my lips. A numbness followed the needle sting, and I tasted blood.

"This one stitch to hold you. To keep you silent. To remind you." She breathed on me. I smelled rot and tree pitch. *"Do not speak of this, un-mortal man. You alone owe me this debt. You alone will pay."*

She pulled her hand back, and I thought I saw a drop of my blood hanging from the thread on her finger.

"And if I do not?" I asked, surprised she had left me with my voice. "If I do not find the St—"

—lightning skipped through my lips, pouring fire down my throat. I was burning—

I gasped, and there was nothing. No pain. But I knew I could not speak of the thing she asked me to find. Not even to her.

I was covered in sweat, freezing.

"If I do not find it?" I said through chattering teeth.

"Then I will tear out what remains of her heart, Lulaah, Lulaah," she singsonged, *"and devour it raw."*

She bit down, and the echo of her snapping jaw cracked back at me from the ceiling, the walls, the floor.

"I promise you nothing," I said.

"*There is no need.*" She glided backward, and was taller, darker, shedding light as if it had been a temporary cloak. "*I take what I want.*"

More hands grabbed me, my upper arms, my thighs, plucking at my clothing, my skin.

I opened my mouth to yell, but another voice cut in.

"Be gone!" the creature that held me roared.

Fingers and hands fell away, then I was moving, stumbling forward, his palm against my throat shifting to the back of my neck, the other hand binding my wrists, pushing me from behind.

"You must go far from here," he said, "and not return. When you find the book, when you find its binding, that which Mother Hush searches for, return. If you return before then, or empty handed, you will be torn and shredded. It will be your death."

His hands dropped away. I nearly fell trying to catch myself on the uneven ground.

"Who are you?" I asked.

The creature was a shadow in the shadow. But he pulled light onto himself, bits and sparks, like stars falling from a low-hung sky, that gathered around him, revealing his form.

He was more man than creature, slimmer and shorter than me. His skin was gray, his eyes tepid orange, his hair long and twisted to fall behind his pointed ears.

I'd have thought him fae, if he hadn't just proved he was acting as a bouncer for the mother of all Hush.

"I am Thrum."

"Are you trapped?" I asked.

It surprised him. "Am I trapped?" He lifted his hands, palm up, fingers straight in a tall cup. Somehow I knew that motion was amusement. "I am not the lost one, man of two souls. I am not the one stitched and bound."

"You said you would keep me safe. She marked me."

His sharp chin tipped to one side so he could regard me through one eye. "Do you not breathe? Do you not stand? Do you not think and feel?"

"I do."

"Then you are safe." He chuckled through bared teeth. "Perhaps not smart." He blew toward me, across his palms, as if freeing a gently-held moth.

I jerked and opened my eyes. The stars wheeled overhead, sparkling through the trees, the moon long since set. Lu pressed against me, her arm over my chest, her head resting on my shoulder, which had gone numb.

Crickets and katydids chirped and chirred, while frogs croaked and chortled in the mud of the river I could smell.

The wind had cooled slightly, and I adjusted the quilt, making sure Lu was covered.

Lorde, who had moved to the other side of Lu, lifted her fuzzy black head to watch me.

Nothing was wrong. Lorde wasn't in high alert. Lu wasn't awake. The night was calm, filled with nature going about its business without fear of a predator nearby.

But my neck felt bruised, my lips swollen. Ankles and wrists hurt too. The chill on my skin warmed like I'd just walked out of cold storage and into the temperate world.

The dream—it had to have been a dream—lingered in snatches of words, flashes of darkness, and the scent of rot and pitch.

In the dream the creatures, no, just one, Mother Hush, wanted me to find something. Something bound?

I frowned as the details slipped like snakes between my fingers.

What had she wanted? A key? No, a book. It could be any book, a different book, but my gut told me it was the same book Cupid was searching for. The book stolen from us. The book we'd vowed to find.

I blew out a shaky breath. It might have only been a dream, my mind working hard to deal with being more alive now than I'd been in years.

But I was not the kind of man lucky enough to only dream his nightmares.

I dragged my hand over my face, wiping away the dusty grit there.

Grit from a cave that should have only been a dream.

Lorde yawned and lay her head back on her paws, but I knew I wouldn't be able to sleep. So I tightened my arm around Lu and watched the stars wheel across the sky until dawn feathered the horizon, sweeping them away.

CHAPTER EIGHT

"I quit." Val leaned against the nearest tree looking as tired as I felt. I sipped the coffee I'd brewed on our small camp stove and grunted.

"Val?" Lu asked. She sat next to me, braiding her hair to one side, finishing the bottom with a rubber band. Her coffee was on the tailgate next to her, steaming into the morning light.

We'd stowed our gear and decided there wasn't anything in this world—not god, nor beast, nor monster—that needed our attention before coffee.

Lorde snuffled around in the brush beneath the trees, moving her way toward the Meramec, a twisty old waterway that flowed around bend and crook for some two hundred eighteen miles.

Lu had turned off the Route last night and taken one of the many trails that were little more than a suggestion into this out-of-the-way stretch of wild green: grasses and brush and trees and water.

"He's here," I said, answering Lu.

"Does he have any other ideas on the rabbit?"

I glanced up at the ghost and raised one eyebrow.

"Tell her I quit. I quit all of it."

I slurped coffee, then swallowed down another gulp because it was going to take caffeine fortification to deal with him.

"Look," I waved my half-empty cup toward Val, "you've made a deal with a god. Good fucking luck quitting that."

Val crossed his arms over his chest and glowered at me. "What's he going to do? Kill me? Already graveside here."

"Death isn't the worst thing a god can do to a man. Or a ghost," I said.

"Is he trying to back out on his deal with Cupid?" Lu asked.

"Yep."

"Bad idea, Val," she said. "You might think being dead keeps you safe from god punishment, but it doesn't." She cradled her mug between her palms. "If you help us find the rabbit, you're off the hook." She took a sip and groaned.

"How do you make this so perfect?" she asked.

I sat a little straighter and gave her a wink. "Secret recipe."

"He measures out the grounds. You probably just pour them in and hope for the best," Val said, but Lu couldn't hear him, and I could very much ignore him.

"Rabbit?" I asked him.

He sighed and leaned his head back against the tree, staring up into the branches. "I feel like I'm missing something obvious. Something that involves the Riggs. But every time I think of those people I get so angry I can't think straight."

"Anger will do that," I said, thinking of the times I'd been in a blind rage when I couldn't affect the living world. Not being alive made some thinking harder. Sometimes it fogged out memories completely.

"Do they own the rabbit?" I asked. "You said you thought it was alive. A pet?"

"It's… No, not like that. I can't." He dropped one hand down to the head of the wolf beside him who stared at me with ghostly eyes. "Pet isn't right. But something."

I took another swig of coffee.

"Anything?" Lu asked.

"He doesn't know. Thinks the Riggs have something to do with it."

"We knew that yesterday. Anything else?"

I yawned and rubbed the back of my neck. I was bruised and sore from what was probably not a dream last night. "Not that he's saying other than the whole 'I quit' thing."

"I said I know the rabbit, but can't remember the rabbit," Val grouched.

"And that he knows the rabbit but doesn't remember it. He's in a terrific mood this morning. Totally swell."

Lu poked me in the ribs, and I knew she meant it to be teasing, but I winced like she'd gone at me with a dull steak knife.

"Shit," she said, drawing her hand back. "I'm sorry, I keep forgetting. I shouldn't touch…"

"No, hey now, wait. You should," I said, stopping her there. "It's not. Not what it's been." I set my cup down and twisted on the tailgate so I could face her. "Lu, I love you. You should touch me anytime you feel like it. No, don't make that face. I know…I know I've been a little twitchy."

She raised one cinnamon eyebrow. In the morning light, her pale skin glowed like moonlight. "A *little* twitchy?"

"Okay," I said. "A lot. Sudden contact or, I don't know, unexpected touch has been hard, and I don't even fucking know why because it's what I want. What I've wanted all these years. This?" I waved at the trees, the sky, the grass, even our dog who was rolling on her back in something foul smelling like a total goofball. "I want all this. I want it. I want you."

"It's okay." She drew her fingers down her braid, as if she wanted to take it apart and remake it, just to have something for her hands to do. "You don't have to apologize. I don't know… It's hard knowing when I'm pushing too much."

"You are not pushing too much. I'm not apologizing for being a mess, here." I tapped my forehead. "I'm saying I'm working on expecting touch to be good, to be wonderful. But the sensations of the living world are still pretty rough waters for me."

"I know." She reached out then pulled her hand back, a wry smile on her lips. "I'll try to keep my hands off all that handsome."

"Don't you dare." I leaned toward her, and she lifted

her face, offering a kiss, her hands pointedly locked at her sides.

I took one of her hands in mine, fitting our fingers together. I waggled my eyebrows, which made her smile, then I caught her lips with mine.

Lu tasted of coffee, the fresh morning air, and everything I'd ever wanted. I deepened the kiss, opening my mouth and encouraging her to let me in. The tension in her softened, and she gave me all of her, letting my tongue explore and taste, while she did the same.

I was reluctant to pull away, but Val cleared his throat, then started whistling some kind of off-key song about lovin', touchin', and squeezin', and it was annoying enough to make me pull away.

"You could kindly fuck off now," I said to him.

Lu chuckled. "What's he doing?"

Val widened his eyes and just kept whistling the Journey song.

"Whistling."

She dragged a fingertip gently across my temple. "Glaring at the ghost isn't going to change what he's doing, and all you'll get out of it are crow's feet."

"You don't like a man with crow's feet?" I asked with mock affront.

"No, I do. Just shows you're alive." It came out like a sigh, like a dream-come-true.

Dream. Something jostled in my memory. Something from last night.

I straightened, but kept our hands joined. "I had a dream. I don't think it was a dream."

"What do you think it was?"

"Magic. Old magic. Maybe the Hush."

Val grunted. "You better tell her about it. I want to hear too."

Her free hand drifted to the scratch on the side of her neck. "What did they do?"

"I was in a cave. It was impossibly dark. I thought I woke up there. No, wait…" I closed my eyes for a minute, chasing a memory.

"Someone woke me. A voice. Told me to run and to…find her. To save the moon." I opened my eyes, and Lu was watching me. Waiting for the rest of it.

"That voice was terrified, like it was running too. Trying to hide. Then there were other voices in the shadows. Too many. By the time I got to my feet, I had the attention of a Hush. I'm sure that's what she was."

I swallowed and pushed the spike of fear and horror of being so close to that thing out of my mind. "She was a monster. Old."

"*The* monster?" Lu asked, wanting to know if the thing in my dream was the monster that had all but killed Lu and me, turning us both into things not quite living.

"No. This one was…powerful. Unafraid of the gods."

"Lots of foolish things are unafraid of the gods," she said.

"She wasn't foolish. Just…old magic. Ancient."

"Did she have a name?"

"Mother Hush."

Lu frowned, but Val whistled, one low note. "That sounds like the Hush. Creatures of magic so old they came from under the earth, soaking through and seeping into ours through cavern and stone."

"What did Val say?" Lu asked.

"Sounds like the Hush to him."

"Did she speak to you? Mother Hush in your not-a-dream?"

"It could have just been a dream."

"It wasn't," both Lu and Val said at the same time.

I glared at Val, and he pointed at Lu. "She agrees with me."

"Brogan, you and I are too old to ignore our gut feelings. It wasn't a dream. What did Mother Hush do?"

"Threaten me."

Lu nodded, having expected that. Like she said, we were old enough to know the ways of monsters.

"She wants me to find a—" Air went solid in my lungs. I was choking and couldn't inhale, couldn't exhale. I heard Lu's voice, felt her hands at a distance on my shoulders.

Somewhere in the back of my mind I marveled at how strong she was as she caught me and guided me down to lie on the truck bed.

I drifted, drowning, numb and unable to even panic.

Then, as quickly as the paralysis had gripped me, it was gone. My breath whooshed out, and I sucked in good, clean air.

Lu's palm on my chest shifted slightly, as did her fingers on my cheek. "There you are. Okay, you're all right now. Keep breathing. You're doing fine."

I was lying on my back, the hazy blue sky a canopy

propped up by the trees. The river sang a soft song of summer and stone and sweet tumbling flow.

"Did Val do this?" Lu asked, her expression shifting from caregiver to killer in a flash.

"It's not always the werewolf's fault," Val groused.

"No," I said, "not Val. I think it's a binding." I licked my lips, waiting to see if I was going to lock up again.

"Do you want some water?" Lu asked.

"No. I'm all right. Let's see if I can figure what triggered that. What was I saying?"

"Mother Hush wanted you to find something."

Just hearing those words, made me break out into a sweat. "Okay. I remember that. And she wants me to…" My arms and legs started to tingle, like I'd gulped down so much air I was about to pass out. I changed tactics. "You know that part, so I'm not going to say it."

"Can you tell me what she wants you to find?"

"Better not," Val said. He was leaning over the side of the truck bed, looking down at me. "You have… something on your mouth."

I lifted my hand and wiped my palm across my lips.

"It's still there." Val leaned closer.

"I don't think I can say it," I told Lu. "Val's staring at my mouth."

"What are you doing, Val?" she asked.

"This would be a lot easier if she could hear me," he said.

"I'll tell her what you say," I said.

"You only tell her the gist. Not what I actually say. I don't usually care, well, I do, but…" He shrugged.

"Right now, though, you're going to want to repeat my words exactly."

"And if I don't?"

"You're going to go stone again, and this time you might not come back in time for all your fleshy bits to still be fleshy."

"Val's an ass," I said to Lu.

She looked around, searching for him. "You know, I have some things around here that can kick ghost ass."

The ghost wolf growled. Val snorted. "Do you want my help or not?"

"It's fine," I told Lu. "He thinks he has something useful. He's ordering me to repeat it exactly."

She brushed her fingers down the side of my face, tips dragging through the scruff of my jaw.

"All right," she said. "I'm listening."

"Lu," Val said.

"Lu," I dutifully repeated.

She just gave me a slow blink.

"Brogan is a total tool."

I looked away from Lu so I could glare at the ghost. "Wanna try that again?"

His smile was sharp, showing teeth much too pointed for a human.

"Brogan is a tool. Go on, say it."

I sighed. "Brogan is a tool. Go on, say it."

He chuckled, and Lu raised her eyebrows.

"He's being used by a Hush."

"He's being used by a Hush," I repeated, feeling stupid. We weren't getting anywhere with this.

"I've heard a story about a man like Brogan," Val said, shifting slightly closer to his wolf so that where they were separate, and where they were whole, blurred. "Say it."

"I've heard a story about a man like Brogan."

"This man was caught by the Hush. Forced to do their bidding. A boon—wait, don't say that word. Say the man did a favor instead."

I repeated it all for Lu.

"To make sure it was done right, there was magic. Something that sews like needle and thread."

I said all that too.

"Now, instead of saying this to her, do this." Val pinched his pointer finger and thumb together, miming holding a needle, then he made looping movements by his lips to indicate sewing. "Not to your lips, but to hers."

I swallowed, my mouth suddenly dry. "I'm going to just do something that adds to his story."

"About some random man captured by some random Hush creature," Lu said. "I'm listening."

I lifted my hand and did the same motions Val had done.

Lu's lips went pale. "Okay. I'm going to ask Val some things. You just tell me his answers.

"Val, did you see this dream thing happen?"

"No."

"No," I repeated.

"Can you see it now? Thread on his lips or some kind of magic?"

"Yes. Thread."

I tried to repeat that and felt my lungs grow heavy. So instead, I nodded.

"Magic?" she asked.

"Yes."

I nodded again.

"That's why the man in your story can't repeat what he's looking for?"

"Yes."

Again, I nodded.

"Does the man in your story know what the Hush asked him to look for?"

Val leaned over me, solid enough, I couldn't see the trees or sky through him. "Do you?"

I turned my focus inward. I could remember the cave, the voices, the Mother Hush. I could remember the magic, the hand of the other creature shoving me around.

But I could not remember what it was she wanted me to find.

I shook my head.

"That's not very helpful, boyo," Val said. "Is it the rabbit?"

"Is it the rabbit?" Lu asked.

"No," I said, "and that's me talking. It's not the rabbit."

"Okay, so we need answers," she said. "We can do that. We can find answers. We know people who know magic. People who have answers."

"Not Crossroads," I whined.

"Absolutely, Crossroads. You don't have to like Erica —Ricky—for us to get information out of her."

"I like her just fine," I lied.

I heaved up so Lu and I were now facing each other, shoulder to shoulder each looking opposite directions but choosing to stare at each other instead. "I just don't like how much she likes you."

She blinked several times, then her eyebrows rose. "That sounds totally reasonable."

"I just…I just think she's a little too happy to see you any time you stop by."

A teasing smile played at the corners of her mouth, and I could tell she was fighting back a grin. "She's only happy to see me because I bake for her."

"I don't think that's it."

She laughed, and I jumped down out of the back of the truck, annoyed I'd admitted even that much. I wasn't jealous.

"Brogan, no," she chuckled, reaching out to grab at my arm. "I just had no idea me being there bothered you. You've never told me before." She hopped out of the truck and slammed the tailgate into place, then dusted her hands.

I strolled off toward Lorde.

"Like I'd waste the little time I had with you talking about Ricky." And, yes, I heard how her name came out of my mouth.

"You could have. If it was bothering you this much, I would have liked to have known. I would have visited her less."

"It didn't matter," I said. "Not enough for me to ask you to stop doing something you liked doing."

"I like her because she knows what I am." She

moved over to the driver's door and opened it so she could lean there half behind it. "I don't have to hide or pretend around her. And she has more information about magic, lore, and supernatural items than I'll ever gather in a lifetime. Several lifetimes."

"Plus she has that fancy kitchen, and you like to bake." I gave her a little smile over my shoulder.

She smiled back. "I do. And this time I get to bake for you."

"Sounds like you're looking forward to that."

"You have no idea how much."

I turned back to our dog because that look on Lu's face, all the heart in her words, was more than a mere mortal like me could bear.

CHAPTER NINE

The front seat springs creaked as Lu settled into place, and then the big door swung shut with a clang. Lu started the engine.

"Lorde," I called, "come here, girl."

Lorde lay flat on her back, all four feet hanging in the air. Her black tongue lolled out of her mouth, and she wagged her tail. Off in the brush behind her, the river sang its endless melody. The smell of mud, green leaves, and warm algae rose to fill my nostrils.

Good smells, living smells. But there was a bit of stink mixed in with it all. Maybe rodent, maybe some other dead critter.

"Such a silly rube," I said to Lorde. "Come on, let's see how badly you reek."

She wriggled in the dirt one last time then stood up and shook, sending a cloud of dust in every direction. Then she trotted over to me, sticking her cold wet nose in my hand.

I petted her and gave her a good scrub behind the ears. She panted, her tail curled up and wagging.

"You stink," I told her, "but not enough to keep you out of the cab. C'mon. We've got a couple hundred miles ahead of us today."

We circled around to the front of the truck. She jumped up onto the seat and I followed.

"Might want to roll the window down," I suggested.

"Why?" Lu said, then she wrinkled her nose. "You know the other good thing about Ricky?" She cranked down the window.

"Nope."

"She has an outdoor bath big enough for Lorde."

I just grunted and stared out the window.

Lu got the truck turned in the right direction, and in fairly short order, the dapple of shade lost out to bigger and bigger patches of sunlight.

"She is useful," Lu said after a while. "Ricky."

I didn't know if she was poking at me just for fun, or if she was checking in, trying to measure where my head was at.

I reached across our smelly dog, and Lu's hand immediately dropped into mine. Our fingers slotted together in the way that was just our own.

"She has her uses," I said.

She kept her eyes on the road, but nodded.

"She gives you a place to bake. I like that."

She nodded again. It looked like it was taking a lot of effort for her to stay silent, for her to keep her eyes on the road, for her to let me talk this out.

"She has more information on magic because she is

a thief and a ne'er-do-well and a, a *pirate* who has never found anyone else's fortune to be out of her reach."

The corner of her lips quirked, as she worked hard to control the smile.

"She's been good company to *you*," I grumbled, "despite her failings."

"She cares about us," Lu added, gaze still on the road. Locked there like none of this mattered all that much to her, like this was a casual conversation instead of what it actually was: us feeling each other out and working to get on the same page.

"She cares about you. She doesn't even know me."

A frown tugged lines between her brows. "I've told her about you, a lot. Years, Brogan. You are all that I've talked to her about for years."

She wasn't wrong. "Still, she's never met me."

We drove a while in the silence, our stinky dog snoring between us.

"You've been there though," she said in a small voice. "You've stayed with me most of the time, haven't you?"

I squeezed her hand gently. "I've been there with you for all of the time. Always."

Tension flowed out of her, and she propped her elbow on the open driver's window. "Because you love me."

"Because I love you."

"And you know Ricky is our friend. Well, my friend, but also yours."

I didn't answer, but instead turned on the radio. Lu

seemed okay with the ceasefire, and we let the road and hours roll by.

It was almost noon by the time we nicked the edge of Joplin and turned south toward the unincorporated community of Hornet where Crossroads lived. It was greener here, the fields clogged up with big trees whose branches arced over the road and threw shadows and light at us like buckets of confetti.

Val had been riding along with us, silent, which was a nice change. But he finally spoke up. "I think I know what the rabbit is."

I turned off the radio. "I'm all ears," I said.

Lu glanced over.

"Valentine," I said.

"I was thinking rabbit, like fur and cotton tail," Val said. "Part of me knew I'd seen a special rabbit, but not a pet like you said before."

"This gonna take all day? Because we're running out of road."

"Maybe I'll keep my mouth shut, let you figure it out, and throw you a thumbs up for a good job in a year or three."

I leaned a shoulder into the passenger door, so I could twist to see him better. "Look at that," I said. "We're both assholes."

Val scowled, and his wolf growled, but it was only a second before his lips quirked up. "I might have liked you when I was alive. Or I might have wanted to punch your face."

"Tell me about the rabbit. You help us, you get your reward from Cupid, whatever that might be."

"Being dead was messing up how I was thinking about it."

I held back a frustrated sigh.

Being dead was a hell of a thing, and ghosts always wanted to talk about it.

"Sometimes my memories feel more real than this." He waved his hand between the two of us. "It took time to sort it all out. I'd seen a rabbit, but special. Worshiped."

"An idol?"

"Right. That's what I was thinking, or maybe a sacred place. River spirit, forest spirit." He shook his head, and suddenly looked very, very sad. "We still have them, you know. Werewolves. Some of us don't pay attention to those things any more, but some do."

He was quiet so I spoke up. "Your people are the Riggs?"

He shook his head, then tipped his head back, exposing his neck. "Pack out near Jefferson City. I left. Burned that bridge until the river went to steam." His mouth twisted in a wry smile. "Threw my lot in with the Riggs who betrayed me, of course."

"Of course?"

"Opposing packs. Outsiders are never welcome."

I shouldn't ask it. It was none of my business. But I was beginning to think there was more than one reason Bo hooked Val up into this journey. Had a feeling that, until the reason for that was solved, we'd be hitched to a ghost for the foreseeable future.

"So why did you leave your pack?"

"A lot of reasons. They left me first, really. Used me

as a sacrifice. No parents. No siblings. Expendable. I didn't fit in."

I waited, both hoping and dreading he'd say more. A mile rolled by on this narrow road, through oak trees and fields of grass. A few clouds mustered to take a run at the sky and evaporated before they got far. Lu squeezed my hand, asking if the conversation was over.

"Who did they sacrifice you to?" I finally asked, gently.

"What," he said. "I think it was a what. Those memories are too bright to stare at too long. I just go blind with rage." His wolf moved closer to him, edges blending, and closer yet, so the wolf's head was centered in his chest, his ghostly eyes burning red.

"They were going to throw me in a cavern, leave me for the spirits to kill."

Lu flicked on the indicator light even though there wasn't anyone behind us for miles. Crossroads was right ahead.

Sometimes folk came out here looking for the Spook Light drifting across the Devil's Promenade, but they never noticed the Crossroads. Whether it was the unassuming location, the twisty old road, or just the steeped-in loneliness of the place, the casually curious moved right on by.

But the truth seekers, the magical, the desperate, always found their way here.

I wondered which of those things we were today.

"They thought giving up one of their own would placate the monsters. Dark spirits have always wandered at the edges of our land. But then food was stolen, and other, random items. A wind chime, a chair, a shed disappeared.

"Then Teddy went missing. Three months old. Couldn't even crawl yet. Somehow got out of a locked house, no windows open."

"Could have been a human break in," I said. "A kidnapper took the baby."

Lu stiffened a little. She hadn't heard Val's side of the conversation.

"No, it wasn't human. It wasn't werewolf either."

"How do you know?" I asked.

"There was no scent of anything, just threads left behind."

I pressed my fingers to my lips.

"Just like those," he said, "woven like a spider web around Teddy's cradle."

"Did they find him? The baby?"

"About a week later. He wasn't harmed, but hasn't shifted into his wolf form since."

"How long ago was this?"

"Three years."

"They got the baby back," I told Lu. She nodded and slowed the truck. We were almost at the Crossroads.

"They wanted to keep everyone safe. I understand that. I wasn't blood related, wasn't really accepted. I overheard them saying they were going to send someone, going to send me to talk to the spirits. It was a sacrifice, *I* was a sacrifice. Expendable.

"I ran. To the Riggs. I thought… I don't know what I thought."

"You were looking for sanctuary. Family. Pack. You

thought the Riggs would take you in. Is that why you want revenge on Danube?"

"I don't want revenge on him. I'm angry at him. Furious. Maybe I wouldn't mind punching him once or twice." He flashed me a sharp smile. "But I want revenge on the Hush who killed me."

"Wait," I said, running his story through my head. "You left the Jefferson City pack three years ago when the baby returned. You ran before they could take you to the caverns, but you said the Hush killed you a year ago. How did you end up in the cavern?"

"Can you believe I volunteered?" He grimaced and ran his fingers down the edge of his black leather vest, the straps of leather and beads on his wrist sliding forward with the movement.

"You volunteered."

"To kill the Hush?" Lu asked.

"Apparently," I said.

"No." His wolf shifted inside him, somehow growing bigger, taking up more space. "Danny—Danube—and I were…friends." His gaze flicked to me and away, and I thought there was something there, something more, but before I could ask, he went on.

"He was kind. He stood up for me. Told Summer I would be a good addition to the Riggs. That I would pull my weight.

"He wasn't wrong. I did my part for the pack. But there was a Shadow they were looking for. It had been taken from someone, or lost its way? I don't remember exactly.

"They thought the Shadow might be hiding in the

caverns. They needed to find it. I know that sounds like a prank you'd pull on a kid, but they were serious. Worried. There are so many caverns, and they'd been searching for a long time. I don't know how long."

"You went into the caverns to find a shadow," I said.

"I went into a lot of caverns. But that last one…I woke up in there. In a cavern. Darkness all around. And I saw him. The Shadow. He wasn't lost. He was trapped. Bound in spider silk. I tried to save him…"

We waited for him to say more. To finish the story. When he didn't, I asked, "The Hush?"

He nodded. "I thought I heard Danny. Thought he was coming to save me." He finally turned his gaze back to me, and there was a wry acknowledgment there. "I was wrong."

We sat with that, his death between us, giving his truth space.

"I'm sorry," I said. "No one deserves that kind of death. Alone and in the dark."

"I wasn't alone. The Shadow was there too. But trapped like me."

"What about the rabbit?" I asked. "You said you remembered something about it."

"I think the rabbit is Abbi."

Lu slowed the truck and brought it to a halt there in the middle of the cracked two-lane road. There was no one coming from behind. Ahead, the road became an intersection where four roads, each facing squarely at the compass points, converged.

The horizon seemed to go on forever around us,

fields of green dotted by old oaks, stretching endlessly into in a blue haze.

In the wedge of land between the road that led west and the road the led south, was a sprawling building that might have been a garage or warehouse a hundred years ago. Shaped in a horseshoe, the gray paint was peeling off the wood slats that reached up three stories from the brick cladding at the base. The windows on each floor cut a slice of sky, reflecting clouds and treetops.

Stuck on one side of the building, was a motel sign that I didn't remember seeing before: an old neon arrow that said TWILIGHT MOTEL.

"What did Val say?" Lu asked.

"He thinks Abbi is a rabbit."

He leaned forward, into our space, bringing a wash of cold with him. "When you say it that way, it sounds ridiculous."

Lu shifted away from that cold, but turned toward him. "Why would Abbi be a rabbit? Is she a shifter?"

"No," Val said. "Not how you're thinking. You know there's a reason us werewolves are so protective of her. She's connected to the moon. I don't know if she's a goddess, exactly, but she's in the legends, the stories. She's the rabbit in the moon."

"What did he say?" Lu asked.

"Abbi's the rabbit in the moon," I said.

Lu blinked. "The rabbit shape we see on the moon?"

I shrugged. "It's not my theory."

"There are stories," Val insisted. "You know, how the rabbit does a good deed and ends up on the moon with a mortar and pestle making immortality juice. Or maybe it's rice cakes?"

"There's stories?" I asked Lu.

"Sure," she said. "Stories about moon goddesses. But the rabbit who goes to the moon isn't a goddess. Or not in the traditional sense. There are stories about that rabbit."

"Do you know them?" I asked.

"Not all of them off hand. But you know who does?"

"Don't say Crossroads."

"Crossroads." She grinned. "And look! That's her place, right up there." She opened her mouth in fake surprise. "We could just walk right in there and ask her."

I pressed my lips together, holding back comments that would only make me sound like an ass. "Fine." I said. "If we have to."

Lu chuckled, a soft sound that brushed over my skin like feathers on silk.

"You are not as subtle as you think you are."

"I never said I was subtle."

She tossed me a smile, then put the truck into gear and took the road west, toward the Crossroads, and hopefully, the answers we needed.

CHAPTER TEN

Lu parked around back, beneath an open carport that held a black truck and bright red hatchback.

Both vehicles belonged to Ricky, and unless someone had hitchhiked in (always possible), she wasn't entertaining any other guests.

Not that a lot of people even knew what this place was.

"Crossroads is a friend of yours? Of hers?" Val asked.

"Hers."

"I've never met her." Val stared out the window. "Bet I'll like her."

"Don't care."

"Bet we'll be best friends. She's gonna like me, Brogan. Best friends."

"What's he saying now?" Lu asked.

"He's just trying to get a rise out of me. Which he won't. I don't care if he's best friends with Crossroads."

Lu nodded, keeping her face carefully neutral. "Good to know."

I shoved the door and shouldered my way out of the cramped space. I twisted my spine to get the stiffness out of my back.

"She's got a hot tub," Lu said, watching me abort the calisthenics.

"I'm fine."

"Your back hurts."

"Little aches and pains make a man remember he's alive," I said.

"Also makes him grumpy." She bumped her shoulder into my arm as I fell into stride next to her. Lorde trotted ahead of both of us, tail wagging, ears pricked up.

"He's always grumpy," Val noted.

"Ghosts make me grumpy," I said.

"And Crossroads," Val added.

"Hold it there, both of you," a voice called from the porch that ran the full back of the place.

We froze. Val kept going though, strolling toward the porch and the woman there.

The woman—Crossroads, Ricky—leaned her broad shoulders against the porch post, resting at an angle that did nothing to disguise her height—six feet, two or so—or her strong, thick body.

Her pine cone-brown hair fell in a shaggy cut around a face with good cheekbones and dimples when she smiled, which she very much was not doing at the moment.

Today, she wore wide leg jeans and a denim shirt

that she'd rolled up to the elbows, exposing the clash of colors and whorls of ink that flooded her skin.

I'd always known the tattoos were magic. I had seen them in action a few times when she was walking the perimeter of her property, walking the compass points of the old roads, setting guards and wards that flared bright, then sank into the ground, the concrete, or the dust, like summer rain.

She was careful about letting anyone see the magic she wielded, but right now, three of the tattoos—the Lapland Longspur on her left elbow, the wisteria vine coiled down that arm, and one of the runes that tumbled across her forearm—glowed with will-o'-the-wisp fire.

"Hello, Ricky," Lu said. We weren't moving. We both knew how powerful she was, especially here on her land.

"Lula," she conceded with a nod. "Who's the man?"

I felt my eyebrows rise. "All these years, and you don't recognize me?"

Val winked out of existence, then appeared in front of Ricky on the porch, standing one step down from her, his wolf still merged with him, ears back, wary.

"What the hell *are* you?" Val asked.

Ricky flinched and raised her arm with the Longspur. The bird's wings flapped slowly as if it were underwater ready to launch into the clear air. Her hand cupped, like she was holding a ball, concentrating magic into it, and her gaze shifted to Val.

"Ghost," Ricky said. "Not now."

"You can hear—" Val said.

Ricky snapped her fingers.

The bird on Ricky's arm flew through the wisteria vines, winging down to the back of her hand, her fingers, beak open in a call I could almost hear.

Then the bird disappeared. So did Val.

"Well, shit." I turned to Lu. "I'm gonna need to get that tattoo."

She grinned. "Why? What did she do?"

"She made Val disappear." I raised my voice. "Oi, who's your artist, and can they get me in next week? I'll pay double."

Lu shook her head. "Like we need to get mixed up in more magic."

"Point," I said, "but you don't have to listen to him all day and all night."

"We've only known him for two days."

"Feels like a lifetime."

Ricky had been watching all this, her cool gaze shifting from Lu, to me, and finally to our joined hands.

I saw the moment she put it all together. Her eyebrows went up, and the magic rolled through all the tattoos, flaring them in soft hues of starlit fire, one by one, from elbows to fingertips.

Then she smiled, revealing those knock-out dimples and a crooked eye tooth. "Brogan Gauge? Do I have the pleasure?"

She pushed away from the post and *thunk*ed down the stairs, her moccasined feet scuffing the old, creaky boards. She took the yard in powerful strides and stuck her hand out as soon as she was in range. "Brogan?"

I shook her hand—firm grip, but she didn't turn it

into a macho test of strength—her moss agate eyes curious.

"Ricky," I said. "Good to meet you."

"And you. All these years." She released my hand and opened her arms for Lu, who, unsurprisingly stepped into her embrace.

"You did it," Ricky muttered into her hair as she held her. "You got him back. I'm so happy for you Lu-lala."

Lu made a little pleased sound that was muffled by their embrace, and then they leaned away from each other, although Ricky still held her by one hand on each shoulder.

Lu was absolutely grinning from ear to ear at her, more than delighted. Giddy.

"How?" Ricky asked. "You've looked for so many years. No, wait. Don't tell me yet. This deserves celebration. Get on in here." She pivoted and draped one arm over Lu's shoulder and reached for me, catching hold of my bicep, then turning so we all faced the house. "We're going to dine, and drink, and you're going to regale me with the stories of your victory."

Lu giggled, and it was a wonderful sound, even if Ricky was the reason for it.

I shifted my arm out of her grip, not liking being touched by her. Maybe it was because I didn't like to be touched. Maybe I just didn't like her.

Or both. It was probably both.

Lorde galumphed ahead of us, trotting up the steps, then sniffed her way down the length of the porch.

"I saw you standing there, and I thought, my Lu-lala

doesn't travel with strange men. Can you believe I was worried he had captured you against your will? I beg your forgiveness for doubting you."

Lu laughed.

The absolute joy Ricky sparked in Lu, her arm, still over Lu's shoulder, friendly, companionable, and certainly welcoming, hit like a mule kick to my gut.

Ricky was her friend. One of the few people she could trust in the world. In one of the few places that felt like a haven to her.

I wasn't jealous.

But the jumble of feelings were hot and twisted: guilt, fear, definitely pain, and it was much too much for me to sort out in front of the two of them.

"Lorde needs a bath," I blurted out. They paused by the door, Ricky having already opened the screen so Lu could pass through.

Lu ducked out from under Ricky's arm, and Ricky shifted, the door still open, but now she stood with the screen to her back.

"Brogan?" Lu's smile was falling, her eyebrows knitting together. All the joy, that giddy freedom gone, flattened under worry for me.

I took a breath, rubbed my thumbs over my fingertips to keep from drawing her against me, behind me, and taking her away so I could keep her as mine. Just mine.

I dug deep for a smile, pulled it into place, and shifted my weight so I was resting on my back foot. Relaxed. Easy.

Some of the lines on her face smoothed.

"Lorde needs that bath," I said. "I could use a little fresh air. Stretch my back."

Her gaze searched my face. "Are you sure?"

I bussed her cheek. "The dog stinks, and I'm not ready to be indoors yet. Go. Have fun."

She considered me for a moment more, then stepped back. "You know where the hose is?"

"Yes."

"And the soap?"

"You still keep it in the shed?" I asked Ricky.

"Shelf on the right." Her smile had something heavy in it, as if she were trying to puzzle me out. As if she wasn't quite sure that she could trust me.

"Got it." I turned and stumped down the steps, calling for Lorde.

The dog bounded after me, her mouth open in a happy smile, her black tongue lolling.

I lowered my hand, and she walked under my fingers, making sure she lifted her head so I could scratch behind her ears. Then she was ahead of me, stopping occasionally to make sure I was still heading in the same direction.

I clicked my tongue for her, and we rounded one of the jags in the building where a room extended past the other on one side, creating a little courtyard hemmed in on three sides.

The hose with an adjustable sprinkler head was attached to one wall. The exposed copper pipes had gone green.

A big cast iron soaking tub that Ricky had scavenged from a late-1800s health spa was set in the ground so that only a short lip of it rose above the bricked patio that surrounded it.

I glanced in the tub. Clean except for a few dried leaves at the bottom.

Big enough to wash pets, shifters, and other such monsters who wandered through here, looking for knowledge, help, and rest.

And plenty big enough for our furry girl.

"Come on, Lorde. Get in the tub, girly."

She sniffed the edge, then to my surprise, jumped in and snuffled around at the leaves in the bottom. I grabbed the jar of soap out of the little built-in closet. As soon as I unscrewed the lid, eucalyptus and juniper filled my nostrils.

I chose the long leashes, leaving behind the stronger restraints and chains—some that gleamed pure silver, some dark as obsidian, some pale rope knotted with pearls and diamonds.

"Just so you don't jump out of here covered in suds, and run out into one of the streets." I attached the leashes to her collar, then to the eye hooks on the walls. I adjusted the spigots, pulling both hot and cold water from the hose.

She wagged her tail slowly, a little uncertain about the hose, but she liked baths well enough, I wasn't worried.

However, I was gonna get soaked if I bent over the tub to reach her. So I shrugged off my shirt, rolled up my pant legs, then stepped into the roomy tub with her.

"Hey, sweetheart," I said, as I knelt and held her collar. "Let's get you un-stunk." I played the water over her fur, then scrubbed my fingers deeper to get through her wooly undercoat to her skin.

Next was soap, and working up a good, thick lather.

I let my mind wander, lost myself to the textures and smells of the warm water against cool cast iron, the splashes of it hitting sun-heated bricks. I lost myself to the fresh herbal scents overtaking the foul stench of whatever Lorde'd rolled in.

I gave my breathing some attention, filling my lungs until they stretched, exhaling slowly. Then I closed my eyes to savor the sun on my bare back, droplets cooled by the licking breeze sliding down to my waistband.

The breeze brought Lu's laughter. Such a rare thing to hear over all these years, it shot through me like an arrow.

She was laughing with Ricky. Happy here. Happy with her. Happy without me.

I gave myself a moment or two to feel that emotion, to be sad and angry and jealous. To be devoured by my pettiness and insecurity.

Lorde licked my knuckles. I opened my eyes and chuckled.

"You look ridiculous. Get you wet and you're a scrawny thing, aren't you? All right. Let's rinse you off."

Rinsing led to shaking, which led to more rinsing, and by the time that was done, I was wetter than she was. I turned the water off and unhooked the leashes. Lorde ran like she'd just escaped certain torture, zooming back and forth across the grassy patch of yard.

I shrugged back into my shirt, put everything away, and strolled to the porch and up the stairs.

Lorde clattered up the stairs on my heels and trotted into the house, pleased with herself.

I followed a little more slowly, crossing the threshold into a wide entryway with faded wallpaper that may have once had a pattern of flowers, or maybe a map of the world, all of it trimmed with dark wood at the edges of coved ceilings.

I dragged my finger along the hallway wall, the scent of the place—a hint of cedar shakes, the waxy honey of polish, and then, a few steps farther in, the full, bold, comforting fragrance of melted butter, sugar, and the deep richness of chocolate and cherries.

Lu chuckled, a soft sound, and then the rise and fall of conversation, two voices, carried me the rest of the way through the narrows of the house. I passed rooms filled with books, shelves stacked with oddities. It was as if someone had wanted to open a museum, but had instead tossed their finds into the bedrooms, dens, and pantries.

A staircase curled upward at the end of the hall. I glanced that way, but stayed on my path, following my nose, following my ears, but mostly, following my heart.

The hall ended at the kitchen which spread the width of the house. It was a beautifully restored space with new, gleaming copper, and stone, and rough-hewn wood running across the rafters.

This space felt older than the rest of the house, even though it carried modern design elements. There was something of the hedge here, of aunties and twigs, inked spells and old stones, soaking up protection and whispered vows.

This was the soul of this place, and in that soul, the magic gathered.

I paused in the doorway. Lu danced, her back toward me, swaying gently with the old radio turned down low, as if that music was meant for her alone. She'd taken the time to re-braid her hair, and now it hung softer around her face, the braid falling in a loose crisscross between her shoulder blades.

She'd tied a towel around her waist and was leaning over the big wooden farm table, kneading dough with her fingers and palms.

Flour covered the table, and one flour hand print dusted the back pocket of her jeans. She picked up the rolling pin and the *clack clack* of the rolling pin kept a steady beat as she worked the dough into the shape she wanted.

The music shifted, something more upbeat, from the 1950s, maybe. No, the 60s. She lifted the rolling pin to do the twist, and I took a step.

Ricky came out of the pantry, be-bopping across the old stone floor, singing along to the song in a gorgeous alto. She was a big woman, and she could move.

Ricky held her hand out for her, and Lu dusted hers before accepting.

Then they were dancing, not the twist, but swing, or maybe hustle, and they both knew it like they'd been dancing together for years, like they had been partners for years.

I leaned back into the shadows of the hall, watching, hurting some, yes, but determined not to interrupt, not to take this joyful moment from her. They pulled close, bodies tilted forward into each other, the moves smooth, hips rocking, feet bouncing as they spread apart, then together again, like wings in flight.

Lu's cheeks were pink, her citrine eyes sparkling, her smile full and unguarded. Ricky added an extra spin at the end, sending Lu out at arm's reach, laughing.

The music changed to a slow song, and Ricky raised an eyebrow. "Maybe foxtrot?"

Lu shook her head and moved back toward the dough she was working on for pies. Berry and pumpkin. "Not if we want these cooked before I start dinner."

"It's good to have you here," Ricky said. "I mean, for dinner, but for just…being here. It's been too long, Lu-lala."

Lu folded the dough, transferring it to the pie pan. "Hasn't been that long."

"Years now. In the neighborhood of three? Four?"

"Have you been lonely? You know there are plenty of people who would love to see you, too. If you invited them."

"I get enough of people stopping by uninvited." Ricky shrugged. "I just miss you."

"You just miss my cooking."

Ricky strolled over to the table and swung down into a chair. She was in profile to me, and I had a moment to remember I was no longer invisible. She would see me if I moved or if she looked over at the shadows in the hall. She might already know I was here, watching her. Watching them.

"I do miss your cooking, but your company is the thing. That's the thing for me. Always has been."

"Nice of you to say."

"And the truth."

Lu's attention was on another ball of dough, pressing it with her palms before applying the rolling pin.

"I love your place, you know that," Lu said. "It's just been a couple rough years. I needed quiet. Space."

"You could have had that here. Quiet and space. I'm good at that. And then you wouldn't have been alone when you didn't want to be."

But she hadn't been alone. I wanted to tell Ricky Lu'd had me. I had been there with her. Always.

"I can take care of myself," said Lu. "Plus, I like being alone."

"Well, I've said it a thousand times, but you know you are always welcome here," Ricky said.

"I know," Lu said. "It always feels like home when I return."

Ricky grinned, those dimples popping, and I knew this was a life Lu had built without me. A place she fit, she belonged. A place that had no room for me.

If I didn't want to ruin it for her, if I didn't want her to regret me coming back to life, I had to get out of there.

CHAPTER ELEVEN

I turned to leave, and Lorde trotted down the hall, her tags jingling, pushing past me and drawing Ricky's and Lu's attention my way.

"Hey," Lu said, looking like sunlight and love, and all the things I'd ever dreamed of. "Come on in, the brownies are almost done."

"Look at you, pretty." Ricky bent and waggled her fingers at Lorde. "I hear someone likes rolling in smelly dead things."

Lorde wagged her tail and grunted happily as Ricky scrubbed her face and behind her ears.

"Brogan?" Lu said. "Chair right over there, if you want."

And what mere mortal could refuse that offer?

"Smells amazing." I emerged from the shadow and strolled into the room. If it were even possible, her smile got brighter.

"You're going to love them," she said, excited. "Coffee?"

"I'll get it," Ricky said. "All around, or ice tea?"

"Ice tea sounds good." I walked behind Lu and dragged my hand across her lower back. She leaned into the touch. Then I took the chair on the opposite side of the table from our host.

"Feel like I've been hearing about you for years," Ricky said.

"Because you have," Lu said.

"Because I have," she agreed. "And now I get to meet the legendary Brogan Gauge." She placed a stoneware cup in front of me, then took the chair to my right, putting herself directly across from Lu.

Lu returned to the pies, gathering bowls, spoons, and fruit, moving around the kitchen like it was hers. In some ways it was.

"Nothing legendary about me."

Ricky's gaze lingered, as if waiting for a punch line. When I said no more, she raised a dark eyebrow. "Humble? Or just underestimating yourself? I've never met another person with the curse you've been living with. And for so many years? Most people would buckle."

I drank tea, cold and barely sweetened. Delicious.

Ricky had done her best to look for solutions to our problems. She'd dug up everything we knew about the magic pocket watch Lu wore. She had helped us figure out how long we could let it count down before the curse kicked us in the teeth.

She had been a loyal friend.

"Not every day was a joyride," I said. "But we're here now and some of that is due to you."

Ricky didn't look nearly as surprised at my comment as Lu did.

"You know a Crossroads helps anyone who darkens their doorstep. But when my Lu-lala, and you," she added, "first showed up, I knew you were something different than I'd seen in a long time."

"Oh?"

"Yep. You were the kind of people I could befriend."

Lu ladled fruit into the pie pan: cherries, fresh picked or maybe frozen from last year's crop. Then she tugged over a muffin tin stuffed with smaller circles of dough, and filled those with cherries too. Individual pies. Likely for Ricky to freeze back and eat later.

Lorde had given up on smelling the baseboards and flopped down on my feet under the table.

"We came here because we need some information," I said.

"What? Not for my delightful company? I am shocked."

"I get it," I mumbled.

"You are the first person who's ever rolled in and had a question they wanted answered."

"Regretting the whole thing now," I said.

"I might just have to get my diary and put little hearts around the date."

"Let the pies burn, Lu," I said. "We're leaving."

Ricky chortled and held out her hand. "No. Not the pies! I'll tell you anything you want to know."

"Nope, it's decided. We're leaving." I made to stand, and Ricky's laugh turned deep and hissy.

"All right, all right." She patted the air, telling me to sit. "Stay. What information do you need?"

"The Hush," I began.

Ricky held her finger up, her eyes wide. The tattoos at her wrist flared, glowed, and seemed to trigger rolling fire up her arm.

"Wait."

Lu stopped searching cupboards. She regarded us both. "I can turn the oven off."

"No." Ricky stood. "It's fine. Just give me a minute." She walked the edges of the room, stopping at intervals to press her fingers into the walls, the door frames.

Symbols flared to life, fueled by the magic she carried under her skin, the old magic of this place, of all the things in it, filling her blood.

Once she had finished the circle, I felt her magic spreading through the house like a circulatory system. Runes and spells written on the old bones of the structure, the weird and weave, stretched like muscles holding safe all within it.

Everything outside this room felt more distant. Even the song on the radio was quieter.

"All right," she said, wiping her hands on her thighs, dragging sparks across the denim. "Tell me what you know about the Hush."

"They attacked Lu. And they were in my dreams. Maybe more than dreams."

Ricky glanced at Lula, and after an extended moment, Lu touched the watch hanging under her shirt. "I don't know if it was the Hush who attacked me, but they wanted this."

"The watch?" Ricky asked.

Lu slipped her fingers under the chain and pulled. Hanging next to the watch like a bolt of frozen lighting, was the silver crow feather key. The key that would unlock the book the hunter had stolen from us.

The book Cupid wanted.

Ricky muttered something that sounded like a curse.

"Do you know what it is?" I asked.

Her body shifted toward me, but her eyes remained on the feather key, like it was a snake about to strike. "Do you?"

"We know it opens a book. A magic book."

She nodded, still unable to look away from the key. "Do you have it? Have you seen the book?"

"No," Lu said, "and yes." She returned the watch and key back under her shirt.

Ricky made her way back to the table and sat. She pulled her cup close, cradling it between her hands. "You don't have the book. Do you know who does?"

"Maybe a hunter," I said. "Or it could be in someone else's hands by now."

Ricky sipped her tea. "The silver crow feather key is said to only open one book. It's possible someone made a copy of the key, cast a fake for fun or profit, but there is a lot of god power radiating off that thing. I don't think it's a copy."

"God power?" Lu said.

"Which god?" I asked.

"Yes, god power," Ricky said. "I don't know which one. Everything I am tells me not to touch that key unless I absolutely have to."

"Why is the key made with god power?" I asked.

She studied me like she'd just watched me tumble off the turnip truck. "Because, Brogan," she said. "The book is made by the gods."

I didn't appreciate her patronizing tone, but chills lifted the hair on my arms. "What kind of book?"

"That," Ricky said, "is a good question. There aren't records. It's barely mentioned in even the oldest texts. One legend says the gods themselves wrote it using their powers. Each page carries a spell never before born into the universe."

"Well, shit," I said.

Lu stepped over and placed her hand on my shoulder. I leaned into her touch.

"Cupid's interested in it," Lu said. "Says he'll help us find it."

"He hasn't asked for the key, though?" Ricky asked.

"No," Lu said. "He knows I have it."

Ricky inhaled and exhaled. "It is never a good thing to catch the attention of the gods. How did you meet Cupid?"

"Bo," I said. "He wants us to call him Bo."

"He found us last month," Lu said. "In Illinois. He wants us to do some things for him, and find some things in exchange for us being alive together."

"Oh, Lu-lala," Ricky said. "Is that how you got Brogan back?"

"It wasn't just me making the deal," she said. "Bo came to us and offered. We both negotiated with him."

"What does he want you to find?"

"Right now?" I said, "a rabbit. He won't give us

details, but we think it might be a moon spirit, a girl named Abbi."

"Moon spirit?"

"The rabbit in the moon," I said.

"Okay," Ricky said. "I can work with that."

Lu's fingers slipped off my shoulder, and she turned to finish putting the large cherry pie and mini pies in the oven.

"Plenty of old tales about the rabbit in the moon," Ricky said. "China, Japan, Korea. Cree. Most of them fall along the line of the rabbit sacrificing itself as food for another traveler—usually a god or someone powerful in disguise—and being rewarded for its sacrifice by being allowed to live on the moon. Some tales talk about the rabbit ending a plague, about it using pestle and mortar to grind up magic elixirs, or pounding rice cakes. There's one story that the rabbit rides a crane to the moon."

"Anything about a rabbit being a little girl living with a bunch of werewolves?" Lu asked.

Ricky snicked air through her teeth and leaned back, placing her fingertips on the edge of the table. She also kicked off her shoes so her feet were square and flat on the floor.

Magic pulsed through the room, the same river green that had lit fire through the protection wards. Only this time there were sparks of gold, like sunlight breaking through the cool surface, dancing through the house and sparking other fires, other rivers of magic.

She stared at the ceiling, the old wood there, the old

plaster, as if she were reading a book or watching a show.

Her magic flowed through the house, that river flowing, and returned to her, channels and avenues searched, sand sifted, rocks tumbled to find the treasures hidden.

"Not that I can see," she said. She was still looking at the ceiling, but I was certain she was seeing beyond it, through it, following the magic as it sorted through all the books, scrolls, tablets, and other magical snips and bits she had stored in this place.

"Why?" Ricky asked, gaze going to Lu. "Have you found one?"

Lu swung in between us, depositing plates of thick chocolate brownies in front of each of us.

"Maybe," she said. "The Riggs have a little girl with them named Abbi."

"A human child?" Ricky asked.

"Whatever Abbi is," I said, "isn't human."

"I don't know anything about an 'Abbi,'" Ricky said. "But I can send out some feelers. I do know I'm going to devour this brownie. It smells amazing, Lu-lala."

"It is amazing," Lu said. "Enjoy. Because once you two finish those, I'm kicking you out so I can get dinner cooking."

Lu leaned down by my shoulder, and the scent of her perfume mixed with the chocolate became something even more delicious, even more alluring.

She kissed my temple. "These brownies are going to flip your wig," she whispered near my ear.

Ricky was already risking a molten bite, but I had a fork and put it to use, carving out a big chunk. I blew on it a couple times, steam curling upward in little wisps, then plonked the brownie in my mouth and chewed.

Food was still new to me. The power of it, the way it could touch my tongue and resonate with the rolling electric pleasure of texture, contrast, taste.

This brownie sang out in me like an entire orchestra. Hot, just this edge of too hot, sweet, heavy, rich. It was comfort, passion, and love.

I shuddered, unable to control my reaction, and savored it in my mouth for longer than I probably should have, chasing that wild sensation.

"Told you." Lu's voice again, warm and intimate near my ear. "Wait until you taste dinner tonight."

Her words were a challenge, teasing, a joy I'd last heard nearly a century ago, when she took over her father's bakery and began to grow it into a successful cafe.

She swayed off to the refrigerator absolutely in her element, and I took a breath, the smile on my face impossible to fight.

I tipped my head down and lost myself to the experience, enjoying every bite until I was picking up crumbs with my fork tine.

"…dick move," Val was saying, had been saying for longer than I realized. "So it'd be nice if you told her not to banish me again, because it sucked."

I drank tea and tuned back into my surroundings: Lu humming to the radio, the scents of baked cherries spiced with something more savory, like sage and walnuts.

Ricky picked up and put down little stones and sticks that acted as some sort of centerpiece on the table.

"Earlier," I said, catching Ricky's attention. "When we showed up. You knew there was a ghost with us."

"Sure," she said.

"He'd like you to not banish him again."

Ricky's eyebrow twitched. "How did he get past my wards?"

I looked over at Val who stood at the side door that led to what I thought might be a mud room.

"She's a Crossroads. They have to accept seekers. And I'm seeking."

"Loophole in your Crossroads contract."

Ricky sighed. "The seeker bit?"

"Yep. You might want to rethink that."

"Can't. I'm a Crossroads. All knowledge here is kept for those who seek. Unfortunately, that means ghosts too."

"Like she's so perfect," Val said. "That creepy blood scroll is contaminating all her crystal tablets. Is there a place I can level a complaint? Some boss or creature or witch above her? Because there is gross mismanagement going on here."

"On second thought," I said, "banishing might make him shut his yap about blood scrolls and cross contamination."

Ricky went very still. "Did he say blood scrolls?"

"Yes."

"Is he speaking now?"

"Caught your attention, didn't I?" Val said. "Suddenly the dead guy's useful. You living people are so judgmental."

"Oh, yeah," I said. "He's talking."

"What is he—no, never mind." She stood. "I'm going to take this out back. Tell him to follow me, will ya?"

"Why? So she can banish me again?"

"Are you banishing him? If you are, I want to watch."

Lu snorted, but continued chopping potatoes into cubes.

"I was thinking more along the line of tuning," Ricky said, as she walked out of the kitchen. "Like an old radio station."

Val didn't move, though his wolf paced back and forth through him. "You trust this woman?" he finally asked me.

"She's a Crossroads. You seem to know what that means."

"I know what people have said."

"Which is?"

His gaze met mine, dark eyes serious. "Some say cursed. Too many promises, too many prices paid in exchange for strange knowledge. Too many mixes and conflicting magics tangled in their brains. Often insane."

"I've heard that."

"But Lu comes here and trusts her as a friend."

"She does."

"Do you?"

I only hesitated a moment. "Yes."

Lu looked over her shoulder.

"I trust Ricky."

She smiled. "She's good people."

"There you go," I said to Val.

Lorde slunk out from under the table and stood behind Lu, her tail wagging.

"Can you take her out for a bit?" Lu asked. "Let her run around before dinner?"

I pushed away from the table and finished off the tea. "C'mon, girl, let's stretch our legs."

It took a couple snaps to turn Lorde's attention away from the possibility of snacks. She followed me out into the back yard.

The heat was thickening now that afternoon was easing into evening. Soon the world would hold its breath for the exhale of night.

I leaned on the porch rail, watching Lord sniff around at the dusty grass, slowly making her way toward the small thicket of trees.

Ricky strolled around the side of the building, the tattoos on her arms flickering with magic. She joined me on the porch.

"Your ghost out there?"

"He doesn't belong to me."

"I don't belong to anyone," Val groused from where he'd appeared, leaning against the same post Ricky had been standing at when we first arrived.

"You're Cupid's, now," I reminded him. "Bound to a god."

"Bound isn't the same as belonging."

"He's here," I said to Ricky.

"So I gathered. All right now. Let's see if this does

the trick." She tugged a fountain pen out of her back pocket and licked the tip of it. I glanced at Lorde who was closing in on the trees, her ears perked up, tail curled high. She'd slowed, having heard some critter out in the long grass.

A rising glow turned my attention back to Ricky. She pressed the nib of the fountain pen on the inside of her forearm, nearer the elbow than the wrist, into the center of a tattoo of a moth. The moth flared bright purple, little licks of black sparking through it. When she lifted the pen, the magic lifted with it, fluttering with tiny lavender wings.

She rolled her arm, and the magic stretched and grew into a thick, purple strand that hung suspended. She undid two buttons on her shirt, revealing a tightly packed collage of ink beneath her collarbones. Each picture seemed to rise and fall, shifting borders to overlay or retreat behind the others like cards being shuffled.

It was the magic of this place she always carried with her, yes, but it was also the magic of this woman.

Crossroads were not common in the world. Those few who existed were tied to a specific place and were receptacles of wild magic that gathered like leaves against the edges of their lands. Only a Crossroads could hold, sort, and use that mix of powers that would destroy any other magic worker. It made them uniquely suited to hold a neutral ground for the supernaturals of the world. Made them uniquely suited to interact and offer sanctuary.

A gnarled tree inked on the right side of her chest

seemed full of birds, then flowers, then animals, then stars as the tattoo flowed through the seasons. She pressed the pen nib to its roots which wrapped around the moon.

With a quick stroke and a whispered word, she drew the purple line through it, then up and across to behind her ear where an old-fashioned TV set—spindly legs, rounded screen, and metal antenna—was inked.

The TV flared with static then cleared to blue sky.

"You got those set up like a dot-to-dot?" I asked.

Ricky tossed me a smile, and there was a light in her eyes that was not exactly sane. "You could say that. What's his name?"

"Valentine."

"Valentine, let me see you. Let me hear you."

Val lifted a couple fingers from where he had his arms crossed over his chest. "Yo. I'm right here."

Ricky shifted her gaze, following Val's voice. "Yup. There you are." Purple flowed bright through her tattoos, then faded. "Valentine, you are seen."

"Oh, so you're what? A medium now? Big fucking deal."

"If I were a medium I'd need inner sight to see you. Easier just to tune you in with magic." Her eyes flared purple.

Val stilled, and if a ghost breathed, he wasn't doing that. His wolf, who had been sitting beside him paced forward, putting itself between Val and Ricky, a low snarl rolling from its chest.

"I'd wondered if you were a shifter," Ricky said. "I thought I felt shifter energy, but Brogan only said ghost."

"Brogan isn't a strong communicator," Val said. "How long will this last? How long will you be able to see me?"

"Until I end it."

Val studied her and there was a change in him, in how he was standing. As if he had been cold and suddenly saw a fire in the night, a place to warm his bones.

Belonging, I realized. He was a ghost, yes, but he was still a werewolf, and werewolves had strong family, strong group, strong pack dynamics.

They needed to belong.

There was hope in Val's eyes. A hope that he had found a home in this place, a friend in Ricky.

"I suppose Val's gonna be welcome to hang around from here on out," I said.

Val's eyes cut my way, then back to Ricky.

"Not that it matters," Val totally lied.

"Funny thing about being a Crossroad." Ricky leaned on the porch rail, her eyes tracking Val, letting him know he was seen, letting him know he was welcome. "I meet many people. I even befriend a few."

"Obviously your tastes are faulty if you call Brogan your friend," Val grumbled, though his eyes were still bright, the opportunity of home softening his features.

"Well, Lu-lala puts up with him." She shrugged. "And I like being around her, so, what's a gal to do?"

"Also standing right here," I groused.

Ricky ignored me, but there was a twinkle in her eyes. "You are welcome here, Valentine. Stay as long as you like."

Val nodded. "Okay. Good. Okay. But I have to help them find the rabbit."

"She's living with the werewolves, right?" Ricky asked.

"Living with, worshiped by, protected," Val said. "She's with the Riggs."

"She likes it there?" Ricky asked.

"She likes them. She's not distressed or hurt."

"And you plan to take Abbi to Cupid?" Ricky asked me.

"Cupid just asked us to find the rabbit and do the right thing. I don't know that taking her away from the weres is the right thing."

"If the god insisted?" Ricky asked.

"If Abbi is the Moon Rabbit, even if she's not, I suppose she has a say in the matter."

"That puts you at odds with a god, my friend."

"It wouldn't be the first time."

Lorde *woofe*d softly. There was something in the trees.

I straightened. So did Ricky.

"What?" Val asked, then he turned to face the yard.

There was motion in the trees, something large, something that had been watching us for a while. Something quiet.

Lorde *woofe*d again, and I was moving, jogging down the steps and across the yard, calling Lorde's name, afraid she was going to run herself into danger.

"Hi, hi, hey!" a voice called out cheerily.

Lorde's tail went into full wag mode, just as I realized Val had spooked his way ahead of me, stopping just short of the trees.

"Hi! I knew we'd find you. I told you we'd find them, Dan."

Before I could process what my instinct was telling me, what my ears were telling me, Abbi, grinning wide and waving, walked out from between the trees, a scowling Danube behind her.

CHAPTER TWELVE

D inner was amazing, and Lu had made plenty
enough to invite Abbi and Danube to sit down
for the meal. Val lingered as we all ate around the
kitchen table, alternately throwing glares at Danube,
and staring off in the middle distance, lost in his own
thoughts.

Ricky didn't seem concerned about the mix of
guests, but she did seem quietly fascinated by Abbi.

Abbi laughed and talked with her mouth full and
acted like a young girl having the time of her life.

I helped with clean up, washing the dishes in the big
farm style sink, my sleeves rolled up, and bubbles up to
my elbows.

Ricky and Danube pitched in on drying and putting
plates away.

When Abbi had been curious about Lu's next dessert
—puffed rice cereal with melted marshmallows made
into squares—Lu had set Abbi to the task of making
them in any shape she wanted. We all gathered in the

sitting room just down the hall where we could keep an eye on the girl through the open doorway.

"Why did you come here?" Lu asked Danube. Lu and I had taken the loveseat, even though we barely fit. I had my arm up over the back to make room for her against me, and she'd thrown one leg over mine.

"Abbi would have come alone," he said. "I caught her sneaking away."

"Does Summer know you're here with her?"

He shrugged. "Abbi left her a note. If Summer wanted to be here, she would be here."

"This is Kearney territory?" I asked.

"Not…here." Danube nodded at Ricky. "Neutral ground. Crossroads."

"This is true," Ricky said. "All may come, but I decide who stays."

"So what are we going to do with Abbi?" I asked. "Other than keep her safe."

"Safe from who?" Danube asked.

"A god sent us to find her—Cupid," Lu said. "Your pack is trying to guard her from something. Hunters?"

The werewolf shook his head. "Hunters don't really bother us. Abbi isn't something anyone is looking for. People look right past her because she's such an annoying child."

Abbi, who had been singing off key in the kitchen, squeaked. "Annoying? You're a meanie head, Dan! I am the great Rabbit in the Moon! Worship me! Bring me offerings!"

The corner of his mouth pulled up in a quick smile. "I'm out of chewing gum," he called back to her.

"I don't even like your delicious watermelon gum." Her voice grew louder as she walked our way. "Moon balls!"

She appeared in the doorway, holding a platter of puffed rice treats. "Squares were too werewolfy." She looked at Danube. "Boring. Squares were boring like werewolves, so I made moon balls."

Danube rolled his eyes like an older brother annoyed by a kid sister.

She circled the room so we could all get a good look at the crispy rice marshmallow treats shaped into balls, some of which she had dipped quarter, half, or full in chocolate. "The best thing about these," she said, "is that they're portable."

"You'll eat them all before we get home," Danube said.

Abbi grinned, her whole face tipped upward. "We're not going home tonight. We're going to save my Shadow."

The mood in the room shifted.

"Damn," Val said. "That's what I was forgetting."

"No," Danube said.

"What happened to your Shadow?" Ricky asked.

"Crossroads," Abbi said, walking over to stand in front of her, "you know my stories, don't you?"

"Some of them," she said, "but not all, gentle Moon Rabbit."

Abbi smiled, but it was sad. "I was too gentle. They took him. I think they wanted me, but they took him."

"Her Shadow," Val said. "That's the Shadow they

were looking for, the one I tried to find in the caverns. Rabbit's Shadow."

"All the strings and spider webs," Abbi said, holding the plate of moon balls in one hand so she could make wiggly spider legs with her other hand. "Running across the sky. I was flying to earth. The strings stuck all over me and I fell. I fell for a long time."

"I thought I was trapped…" She swallowed. "But Hado said he wouldn't let them hurt me. He is my friend." Her eyes were watery, but they were also very, very old. Ancient. "My guardian. They took him away. I was fast, but he was faster. I was brave, but he was braver."

"Hado is your Shadow?" Lu asked.

Danube was still scowling at Abbi. "We are not going into the caves."

"We have to. We have to tonight," she insisted. "It's the right sky. The new moon. It's what we've been waiting for, isn't it? It's why the pack hasn't gone into the caves with me yet?"

The werewolf shifted his feet and avoided direct eye contact.

"You said…" Abbi frowned, and it was betrayal in her voice when she finished, "…you said you would *help* me."

"We did. We had been looking for months before you found us. For years. We will continue to look," Danube said. "But we cannot let you go down into those caverns. We can't lose you, goddess."

"I'm not a goddess." Abbi took a deep breath, roughened a little by unspent tears.

When she spoke again, her shoulders were back, her head tilted upward. Proud and so much more than just a child with the moon in her eyes.

"I am not innocent or weak, Danube, even if you see me that way. I am more. A power. A legend. Blessed by gods, cradled by the moon. I am so much older than you, than any of you," she nodded toward Ricky, "even if I choose this body." She pointed a finger that still had a little chocolate on it at her chest. "But I am not a goddess, either."

"It's a trap, Abbi," Danube said. "They want you to find him. They want you near enough they can take you this time. Then they will use you, Abbi, however they want."

She pulled her bottom lip between her teeth. "Maybe," she admitted. "But I don't want anyone putting their lives on the line for mine."

"It is an honor—"

"Danube," she scolded gently. "I know my Shadow. I can find him. No one else can, not as quickly. I don't want to go alone, and I won't turn away help, but if you decide not to go, then I'll go by myself. This is my best chance. Maybe my only chance."

Danube growled, a nearly sub-audible sound, and Lorde, who had been lounging at Ricky's feet, lifted her head and stared at him.

"Will you go with me?" Abbi asked. "I won't be mad if you say no."

He closed his eyes. When he opened them again, they shone red. "I will go with you."

Abbi smiled and looked so very young. "Thank you. Will anyone else go with us?"

Ricky shook her head. "I won't go in those caves. Can't if I'm going to be of any help to you. I can drive you there. I can help you find the way home."

"We're going with you," I said. "Lu and I."

Abbi nodded, her eyes searching and finding Val. "Valentine?"

He straightened, surprised. "Of course I'll go. I tried once, on my own. I think I found him then. It's not far away. Near the Meramac."

She broke out a huge smile. "I'm so excited! We'll find him. I know we will. I'll get some bags for the moon balls." She trotted into the kitchen and began opening and closing cupboards.

"This is a terrible idea," Danube said.

"Probably," I agreed. "Won't be the first we've had. I don't suppose you have any weapons or protection against the Hush?" I asked Ricky.

She ran fingers through her shaggy hair, leaving some of it stuck up a bit. "I do." She stood and stared at the ceiling again, as if reading the contents in the crannies of the entire house written on pages up there.

"Let me see what I can pull together." She left the room and, interestingly, Val spooked off to follow her.

That left me and Lu and the angry werewolf, all of us listening to Abbi's off-key warble as she sang along to the radio.

"She has a terrible singing voice," I noted.

Danube flashed me a fast grin. "She does." He

finally moved away from the wall, closing the distance between us.

"I shouldn't have let her come here."

"Could you have stopped her?" Lu asked.

He considered it, then his shoulders slumped. "No. But the pack will be furious."

"You could call them. Bring them into this," I said.

He exhaled and shook his head. "She didn't want them here. She didn't think they would help. She may have been right. Fewer people going into the caverns will be less noticeable. Maybe we'll finally find him and bring him out without waking the Hush."

"But if we lose her…"

"We won't," I said. "I promise."

"These are old hills, Brogan Gauge, and even older magics move within them. Don't promise what you can't deliver." He turned toward the kitchen, and soon was helping Abbi open and close doors, looking for those bags.

"I don't like you going back in those caverns," Lu said.

"I wasn't really there. I was dreaming."

"Dreams are real, Brogan. So is the dream realm."

I shifted so she fell into me more, and she went with the motion, resting her head on my shoulder.

"I don't like you going either," I said.

"I can take care of myself." She was tight, ready for a fight.

I inhaled, held it, then rubbed my thumb over her shoulder until I felt her relax slightly. "I know you can. I still don't like you going, so we're even."

She nodded.

"This might be the part Bo wants us to do," I said. "The 'right thing' he's trusting we'll know."

"If we should even trust Bo," she said. "He knew what that book was. God powers? God spells? Why wouldn't he tell us?"

I just hummed, because right now, there were too many unknowns for me to see the whole picture.

Abbi sang louder and Danube told her she was killing his will to live. She upped the volume on the radio so she could shout the lyrics, which made Danube groan. There was the sound of a tussle, and I felt Lu stiffen in my arms.

I rubbed the side of her shoulder, then Abbi's cackling laugh rose in victory.

Lu relaxed.

The radio played on, Abbi still singing, using all the wrong words and notes possible.

T he night air through the truck's window smelled clean and growing, like water flowing over rocks still heated from the day.

Lu had parked Silver next to Ricky's black truck and turned off the engine.

I could hear, but not see, the Meramac River that ran close by, tunneling through caves and hollows, winding its way slowly through the hungry green.

"I need you to be careful," Lu said.

"I will be careful."

"You're not just a spirit any more. You bleed, Brogan."

"I know. I need you to be careful. I can't protect you like I could when I was a spirit."

"I've been taking care of myself for years," she said, the edge in her voice a surprise. "I don't need you to take care of me now."

By the widening of her eyes, she realized what she was saying just as the words escaped her mouth.

A part of me was afraid of what those words meant. Was she tired of me being with her? Did she want me to leave her alone?

But I'd been with her for almost a hundred years. I knew exactly what fear looked like on her. Knew what it sounded like.

"I didn't mean it the way it came out," she said.

I reached over and caught the bottom of her chin, turning her face to me. "I love you. I trust you. We are both going to be careful."

She nodded, the shadows smudging her sharp features so that, for a moment, I could wonder if this were a dream.

Knuckles rapped on Lu's window, and I jerked. Ricky gestured for us to come outside.

"Ready?" I asked.

"I am." Lu slipped out the door, shutting it as quietly as possible.

"Bo," I said, my voice low, my hand on the door handle. "If you're watching this, if we're doing the right thing, I'd like to know you'll step up if things go to hell."

Nothing but the burble of the river answered me, so I opened the door and stepped into the night.

Brogan," Ricky said. "I have a weapon for you."

Lu was holding a very short, thick blade no longer than her palm. I would have said it wasn't going to do her much good, but then she shifted her grip on it, and magic flared red, making the blade glow.

"These should at least stop the Hush," Ricky said. "Even if they won't kill them." She had a satchel over one shoulder. From it, she pulled a metal rod. The rod was thicker at one end and pointed at the other—more of a vampire stake than a wand.

"I don't think this will harm you. But you are not quite human and have a magic of your own, I suspect." She held out the rod. "Careful. Just a finger first."

"Don't know why she gets a blade and all I get is a stick…" I grabbed the rod before she could pull it back. A lash of heat and of sound rumbled through my bones, like a storm building inside my blood and muscles.

It didn't hurt, but it was…strong.

"That's what I thought," Ricky said. "You're connected to magic, to the spirit realm, but not made of shadow like the Hush. Good to know. That 'stick' is a lightning rod for magic. Focus your will, and it should blow the flames out of hell."

Chills rolled over my skin and fear soured my stomach and throat. The nightmare of the Hush rushed back: wrists and ankles shackled, a hand pinning my throat while the Mother stitched my lips shut.

"We need to go," Abbi piped up. She had a knapsack across her chest and a dark knitted cap over her white hair. She looked like a tiny smuggler ready to hit the docks.

"Are you staying out here?" Val asked Ricky.

"I'd be a liability in there. All my magic is too visible."

"I can stay out here with you," Val offered. "I'll head in after them in a minute."

Abbi fidgeted from foot to foot. "Now, Danube. We need to go now. My Shadow's in there. I know it. I can feel him."

"You stay close to me," he warned.

Abbi just gave him a crazy, little-kid grin and grabbed my hand. "I'll stay with Brogan. Just in case you try to pick me up and throw me over your shoulder for my own good."

"Once," he sighed. "I only did that once."

She snorted, and Danube palmed her head, gripping her with his fingers and giving her a little shake. "Don't be stupid. Be safe. I'll go first." He strode past us, toward the mouth of the cavern, every inch the protective big brother wolf.

"Hold on tight, okay?" I said to Abbi.

She nodded.

I looked over at Lu. There was a wicked glint in her eyes, and a set to her jaw and shoulders I'd seen a hundred times.

She wasn't afraid of danger, wasn't afraid of a fight. "Maybe you should stay out here with Ricky," she said.

"Who?" I asked. "Abbi?"

"You, Brogan. Maybe you should stay back."

I laughed, the reaction instant, the sound punching out before I could stop it.

She frowned.

"Not a chance," I said. "Not ever. Certainly not now. Life, death, heaven, or hell. Into the cavern of the Hush. I go with you."

She shivered, just once, as if throwing off one emotion for another.

"Together," I said.

"Together," she repeated.

We followed Danube, moving quietly through the dry grass to the mouth of the cave.

The Meramac Caverns were a tourist destination, really one of the original tourist traps, and a big pusher of bumper sticker advertising. You could see the place advertised for miles, the name written on billboards and barn roofs. After all these years it was still going strong.

A gift shop fronted it, and beyond and down, the huge first cavern was rented out for weddings and high school dances. Tours were offered daily, with a nice little patriotic film shown at the end.

But that wasn't exactly where we were going. There was a hidden entrance—more than one—that led to all the unused tunnels, the hidden caverns, if you knew how to look for them.

Danube knew how to look for them.

He pushed between bushes and slipped from sight.

I took a step forward, but then Lu's hand was on my shoulder, as she moved in front of me. Deadly, calm, she stalked through the brush and into the cave.

Abbi squeezed my hand tighter. "I'm scared."

Her face was turned up, her eyes huge and dark, endless pools where stars dipped and glistened.

"You can be afraid," I said, "but I'll look after you. I won't let anything hurt you."

"Promise?" she said in a voice so small, it squeezed my heart.

"I promise."

She nodded, and though her eyes were still wide, and her grip on my hand still tight, she took a step forward.

I pushed the bushes out of the way for both of us, then we ducked into the narrow crack in the side of the hill.

CHAPTER THIRTEEN

The darkness was so complete, it felt like I'd pressed my face against a cool wall. I blinked hard, impatient for my eyes to adjust to the lack of light.

Abbi tugged on my hand. "This way," she whispered, as she slipped around and led me forward, nothing more than a slightly lighter blob of darkness in the darkness.

I strained to hear Lu's footsteps, to hear Danube. I knew they were ahead of us, and this narrow passage only allowed one way forward, but I could not see or hear them in the crush of stone and silence.

"This way, this way," Abbi whispered again, her soft words making more sound than even her feet, or my tight shoes on the stone.

For a moment, I felt like I was a spirit again, floating instead of touching earth, caught in that in-between, in a darkness where no other living things existed. Then a blazing slash of red broke the blackness—Lu's dagger moving before she closed her palm over it again to dampen it—and knew I was here, in this world, the living world.

I inhaled the rot and pitch scent of the Hush. I nearly choked, my heart banging against my bones, warning. There was evil here. A nest, a swarm, and we were walking straight toward the fanged center of it.

"Abbi," I whispered, but my throat was too dry to make the words.

We'd gone too far into the hills. I could see, just barely, but enough to know there were other paths now, holes punched out of the walls, low near our feet, too small for me to fit inside, but not too small for the Hush.

Abbi was still talking, maybe a whisper, maybe a shout, all of it damped, pillowed out, and softened by the pressing stone and darkness.

"Abbi," I tried again, louder, as she tugged harder on my hand.

"Here, here," she said. "He's here. I can hear him." She yanked, and I took a step with her, but tried to draw her back at the same time, feeling the strain, the lengthening of her body as she pulled away from me.

"Don't let go, Abbi," I said. "I can't fit in those holes. You need to stay with me."

A flash of green light blinded me. I hissed and covered my eyes, a slap of pain rocking through my brain.

"He's here, he's here!" Abbi slipped out of my hold, crouched like a little crab, and disappeared into a low tunnel in the wall.

"Wait, Abbi! No!" I shouted, my words falling dead in the air.

The green light dimmed enough, I could see we were at an intersection. To the right of me, the path diverted around a huge stone that had sheared off the wall. To the left, the ceiling jagged down almost to the floor. Above me were stalactites born wet thousands of years ago and still not dried out.

"Abbi? Abbi!" I crouched and tried to peer into the tunnel. It was empty. She was gone.

"Brogan," Lu was suddenly there, her hand on my shoulder. "We have to go. Now!"

The Hush clattered down from the ceiling, skittering across the stalactites, jumping from shadow to shadow. The walls rattled with bones and carapaces wrapped in sticky magic that pulsated like spider silk breathing.

They were descending so quickly, I almost couldn't clock their movements.

"Now, Brogan, now!" Lu pulled me up. But before I could take a step I was hit from above by something heavy that knocked me to my knees.

I tasted dirt and blood as I twisted, striking at the thing on my back with the lightning rod.

Magic crackled under my palm and the rod flashed. The Hush shrieked and fell away, but not before more and more took its place.

I was buried beneath bodies. Hands and claws scratched and dug for purchase. Spider-silk magic wrapped my fingers, my neck, my feet, choking, pulling, blinding.

I could hear the battle around me, even as I strained and struggled to drag myself out from under the creatures.

Danube snarled, throwing the Hush off like a wolf shaking off rain.

I tried to get a bead on Lu. She was a blur of deadly grace, moving faster than any human being, the blade painting red fire, Hush screaming as they extinguished into smoke and oil and darkness.

But no matter how fast she sliced, no matter how many creatures Danube fought, an endless stream of Hush poured down from above.

We couldn't win here, couldn't take a stand.

I wrenched my arm free, stabbed the lightning rod upward, and sent all my fury into the weapon. The lightning rod sizzled with silver magic.

"Run!" I yelled. Lightning arced from the weapon and exploded across the ceiling, illuminating a million hungry eyes. The Hush fell off me, screeching in pain.

Lu grabbed my shirt and hauled me to my feet. Her heat behind me was solid and real, her breath coming fast.

The lightning still pouring from the rod grew brighter—painfully bright—then broke with a smash of thunder.

Into that sudden darkness, we ran.

I could feel her—

—*Lu*—

—sprinting, her feet hitting stone and dust, dodging obstacles she could see, but I could not.

A flash to one side—quick and white—

—*Abbi?*—

—gone faster than I could track, running too, but not pacing us.

"Abbi." I grunted as my shoulder crashed painfully into stone. I overcorrected, my damn tight shoes slid, and I slammed my hip into something on the other side. I swore. "Abbi ran. She's lost."

"We'll find her," Lu said over Danube's growl which rose from behind me as he snarled and snapped at anything that drew close.

We ran.

I huffed air in and out of aching lungs, hit my arms, my thighs so many times I lost count. I stumbled over the uneven ground, wishing I'd listened to Lu and bought good shoes as she led us deeper, or maybe farther, hopefully farther out of the cavern.

A flash of white made me turn my head again, but it ducked away, disappeared before I could tell if it was Abbi, or the Hush trying to play us toward a trap. I thought I caught sight of her again, white hair, wide eyes, but she was smothered in darkness before I could even reach out for her.

We ran. Faster, though my lungs burned. Faster, though my legs shook. Faster, though panic and fear screamed through my mind.

Lu's hand was tight in mine, my footsteps fell in the same rhythm as hers, my eyes stinging with sweat.

I thought I felt a wisp of wind—cool and green, the sigh of river and rain—then the air turned to dust and stone and sweat again.

Lu gasped, her grip jerked. I threw my weight backward, landing hard on my ass, one foot kicking out over the crumbling edge of stone she had almost fallen over.

"Stairs," Lu grit out, pain in her voice. "Down." She

pulled. I stood, my free hand searching for a wall to one side and not finding it, my heart pounding in my ears.

"Fucking hate the dark," I growled.

Lu squeezed my hand, already descending. The stairs jagged right, then left, then we were on a level platform.

"Out," I said. "We need a way out."

"Brogan!" Lu warned.

Two things happened at once: every muscle in my body froze, and the entire chamber lit with a soft blue glow.

Mother Hush swayed out of the shadows, stones and leaves clattering as she moved, glowing lichen casting her face in watery luminescence.

Her eyes were enormous, endless pools of ink glittering with gold that gathered and extinguished, stars drowning in the long night.

"Here you have come to me, broken dreamer, BroGan Gaayge."

I wanted to run. I wanted to pull Lu behind me. But here, in the center of this hill, I was caught tighter than a fly in a web.

"Here is the key, so near her heart, Lulaaah, Lulaaah."

Mother Hush was close now, larger than life, larger than my dream, easily ten feet tall. She bent toward me to look down upon us, her prey.

"Have you found the book? Have you found our Strange weave?" Her eyes flooded with gold that drained away, leaving behind glassy voids. *"No, un-mortal, you have not."*

Eyes and teeth flashed in the shadows. Danube might be nearby, but I couldn't turn my head to see him.

"*This task, you have failed.*" Too many long fingers on one hand wriggled like worms, sticky gloss hanging from each digit.

"*Now, you suffer.*"

My mind raced, the memories of her words in the dream swamped me. She would hurt Lu. She would eat her heart.

No, no, no!

"*Watch her pain,*" Mother Hush cooed. "*Watch her life devoured.*"

I yelled, but not a sound passed my lips. I fought, but not a muscle moved.

From the corner of my eye, I spotted Danube. He was a big wolf, and in the uncertain light, the lighter patch on his chest and one foot shone.

He was locked in a frozen stance, ears back, teeth bared, tail stiff.

Lula, in front of me looked unafraid. Her eyes were narrowed, her stance loose, the dagger in her hand radiating a soft red light.

She was just as frozen as I was, and I wondered if she was screaming inside her mind. I wondered if she was terrified.

If so, it did not show.

Mother Hush bent lower, gliding forward on hidden feet toward Lu, until her huge head, her enormous eyes were only inches from Lu's face.

"*Devour your heart?*" Mother Hush sang. "*So sour, so small, so hard. But there are other ways to heat myself with your blood.*" Her other hand lifted, the claw heavy and black, tapered to razor pincers. She rested those pincers against Lu's chest, and pressed.

I roared. I raged. But was silenced by stone.

There was no blood, and Lu's expression hadn't changed.

Why wasn't she bleeding?

Mother Hush sank her claw into Lu's chest, all the way in, up to her elbow. It should have skewered her, should have shoved all the way through to exit her back.

But somehow, Mother Hush pressed closer and closer to Lu, folding down, compacting. As she became smaller, stones and leaves shed off of her, pinging against the rocky floor like hail in a forest.

She wasn't trying to cut Lu open. It was worse. Much worse.

She was stepping *into* her, possessing her like a ghost.

A single blood tear fell from the corner of Lu's eye. With massive effort, she shifted her gaze to me.

I yelled, utterly helpless, as Lu was invaded, possessed.

A flash of claw leaped into my peripheral vision. I thought it was more Hush come to feast.

But it was not the Hush. It was a wolf, ghostly bright and angry as hell.

Valentine snarled and jumped *into* Lu.

A flash of oily blue light shot out of the top of Lu's head, screaming as it flew.

Lu collapsed onto the floor, and I lunged for her, stumbling as the bindings broke with electric snaps that burned my flesh.

I caught myself with my arms on either side of Lu.

If this was it, if she were gone, I would kill every Hush I could reach, before I followed her to Death's doorway.

But I knew—

—*my tattered soul in her*—

—her heart beat—

—*her tattered soul in me*—

—her soft exhale—

—she was alive.

I pulled her into my arms and stood on legs that barely held.

Val was nowhere to be seen, but Danube snarled and pushed at my leg before leaping ahead of me down a path we had not taken yet.

I stumbled after him, my mind blank with rage, because rage was better than panic.

The nightmare closed around me and time slipped. It was everything I could do to put one foot in front of the other.

I thought I'd lost Danube, but the wolf growled and nudged my hip, leading me as best he could.

And then there was light…

"What in the hell happened? Brogan. Here. Bring her here."

…and there were hands…

"I got her, I got her. Easy, easy. Brogan, you need to listen to me." A woman's voice. I knew her.

"Open your eyes, Brogan. You're safe."

…and then there was the world again.

I opened my eyes. I stood next to Ricky's truck, Lu still in my arms, held close to my chest. I was sweating, freezing.

The wind licked across my skin, and I shuddered beneath the green of it.

"You're bleeding," Ricky said, her gaze on Lu, fingers pressed to her throat where I knew her pulse beat weakly.

"I'm fine." My voice cracked, and I swallowed, making my throat sting. My head was foggy, thoughts sluggish.

But all that mattered was Lu's heart, beating.

"…you can let go, Brogan," Ricky had been saying. "I got her."

I blinked hard and focused on the Crossroads. She had opened the back of her truck and her hands were right next to mine, ready to take Lu.

"She's cold," I said, as she trembled.

"She's not cold," Ricky said gently. "Your arms are shaking. How about we both get her into the truck so we can assess her injuries. And yours."

"I'm fine."

"You're not."

I held her gaze for a moment then looked away to the mattress with a bright chevron wool blanket thrown across it.

I tried to take a step, and my calf charley-horsed.

Ricky just shook her head. "All right, hero. I'm taking her out of your arms. No, don't glare death at me. You need more work than she does. Just…stay."

She shifted her grip on Lu and lifted. My hands slid away from Lu's warmth, then fell to my sides, absolutely exhausted.

Ricky was strong and swung the much smaller Lu

easily into the truck's covered bed. She arranged Lu's hands and legs so she was comfortable and pulled another blanket over her.

I suddenly realized Lorde was barking and looked around, panicked she was being chased by the Hush.

"Had to put her in your truck. She was trying to run down that hole after you," Ricky said. "It's unlocked, and the window's down a bit. I'm sure she wants to see you."

I was already walking to her.

Lorde paced inside, whining and barking and trying to push her nose out the window. I opened the door, still in a daze, wondering if I were alive. Wondering if this was real.

She rushed into my arms, licking and whining. When I finally lifted my arms, she pressed against me, resting her head on my shoulder, breathing.

I threaded my hands into her fur, holding tight to the heat and softness just beneath the coarse outer layer.

And if I sobbed, if I shuddered, trying to shed the horror, trying to shed my fear and helplessness, she did not move.

Her tail wagged softly once, then stilled as she gave me more of her weight. I leaned into her, burying my face in her fur, breathing in her steady, loyal comfort.

"Now you," Ricky said, pressing her palm carefully on my back. I winced from the heat, from the contact, the world suddenly too many hard edges for me to endure.

"Let's get the shirt off so I can see the damage. I'll be careful."

I released my grip on Lorde, and her tail wagged slowly again. I wiped my face with one hand, then straightened and undid the buttons on the shirt, shrugging out of it with a moan.

Everything hurt.

Ricky grunted, her fingers on my shoulder holding me in place while she inspected my back. "You look like you've been through a thresher. Turn."

I turned, and she gave my chest and stomach a look, prodding at my ribs.

I hissed, and she grunted again.

"The cuts and bites all look shallow. You've fractured a rib or two. You're going to be more bruise than flesh by morning. How are your arms?"

I lifted them, turned my hands, clenched and unclenched my fists. My fingers were bruised and scraped like I'd fallen out of a train and come to a stop across a couple miles of gravel.

"Functional." I cleared my throat. "It all hurts."

"I want to clean those cuts. Messing with fae magic or Hush magic is nothing to let linger. How are your legs?"

"Not broken."

"All right, come over here so I can wash your wounds."

"Lu..."

"She's still sleeping. I tended her cuts—not nearly as many as you have and no broken bones I can see."

There was more, more I needed to remember, but thoughts slid from one to the next, none solid enough for me to hold.

"This won't sting, but you'll taste mint. That's how it is for me. Some taste licorice." Ricky had maneuvered me to the back of Silver, where a dented green thermos, sponge, and towel waited.

She picked up the thermos. "Tip forward so I can pour this over your head."

I did so, my breath hitching at the pain. Warm water poured over my scalp sending goosebumps down my spine.

"Now up."

She poured the thermos over the sponge. With quick, careful strokes, she squeezed the water over my skin, from neck to belt, then down my arms, paying close attention to my bloody knuckles.

"Looks like the Hush tried to eat you," she said quietly.

"Lu," I said catching at memories. "Mother Hush possessed her. I thought… I thought…"

"You can stop thinking now. She's alive." She squeezed the sponge to clear the blood and re-wet it. "Now the shoes and pants. I want to see your legs."

I pried off my shoes with a groan and dropped my trousers. The coolness of the sky and heat from the earth wicked across my skin, comforting and clean.

Ricky grumbled and poured more water, sponging a cut on my thigh, scrapes on my hips, and my abraded knees until the thermos was almost empty.

"Your feet are a mess," she said, finishing off the last of the liquid by pouring it over both my feet in turn. "The only thing those shoes are good for is burning. You need boots."

I just glared at the shoes. "Don't have boots."

She made a soft sound and replaced the stopper in the mouth of the thermos. "Mint?"

"Strawberries," I said, swallowing the flavor. I dragged my pants back up and left the shoes on the ground.

"That's a new one. Where's Abbi?" she asked.

"We lost her. I lost her."

She hummed. "Danube left," she said. "Or I assume he was the werewolf running like the fires of hell were licking his tail." She handed me a canteen, and I drank from it, the water slightly metallic, but soothing.

"Don't drink it all. I don't think you have a concussion, but I don't want to clean up your sick if you do."

I gulped down several more mouthfuls then capped it. "Have you seen Val?"

"No." Ricky handed me the towel. I dried off as best I could and pulled on my filthy shirt.

The memory of what had just happened finally cut through the fog. "He jumped. Val jumped into Lu. He fought Mother Hush and forced her out."

We both glanced over at Lu. Lorde had hopped up into the truck bed to curl up beside her.

"Think he's still in there?" Ricky asked.

I used to know these things. Used to be the doorway through which any kind of ghost could touch Lu.

I stepped over and pressed my shaking hand on Lu's wrist. I might not be spirit, but I could still see things, could still feel Lu's heart, her soul.

"You're going to be okay, love," I told her as I looked for any signs of Val or Hush inside her. "We're going to take you back to Ricky's. Get you in a soft bed. Everything will look better in the morning."

She didn't move, but nothing else in her seemed to stir either.

"I don't think Val's still possessing her."

"I haven't seen him with us," Ricky said.

I checked our surroundings. We were still in the same pullout beneath the trees, grass dark against the night, river murmuring, with only the lanterns Ricky had set out giving light to see by.

"No. I don't see him." I stared at the other side of the road where we had entered the cave. Abbi was in there somewhere. I couldn't leave her behind.

I took a step.

Ricky's hand landed on my shoulder. "Hold up."

"Abbi," I said.

"She's not a child, Brogan. You need to remember that. She is the spirit of the Moon Rabbit. Ancient."

"The Hush will tear her apart."

"I'm not saying we don't go in after her. I'm just saying we go in with a plan, with weapons or tools that work a hell of a lot better than what I armed you with."

"They worked," I said. "The weapons. But there were just too many Hush. I think they were waiting for us."

She turned her head and spit. "Let's not give them a second chance to have the upper hand. We go back to the Crossroads, and I'll summon some help. Something I should have done in the first place."

She manhandled me toward her truck, but I dug my heels in. "I'll drive Silver."

"That's a monumentally stupid idea."

But it was Lu's truck. She loved that thing. We'd been together for a month, solid and real in that truck, had made love in the back of it under starry skies and secluded woods.

She'd be gutted if it got stolen.

"I'm driving the truck."

Ricky must have seen something in my expression because she just shook her head. "Follow close. If you decide to drive into a ditch, make it a shallow one."

She strode to her vehicle, and I swung into the cab of mine, shutting the door. It smelled of Lu's perfume, and my chest cramped with fear.

"She'll be fine," I said. "I can feel her. She is very much alive. She's going to be fine."

I turned the keys and wiped the back of my hand over my eyes. Ricky pulled out first, going slow in case I really did try to drive into a ditch.

But I held the wheel steady at ten and two, kept my eyes on the truck, and followed Ricky home.

CHAPTER FOURTEEN

I did not expect the werewolves.

The Crossroads was the same as it ever was, but the ground around it was covered in milling werewolves, some in human form, some in wolf, and a few in that rarer in-between state that fills books and horror shows.

If it was a single pack, it was a hell of a big one.

Neither the Kearneys nor Riggs had that many adult members—there were no children here.

Ricky guided her truck into the garage. I parked behind it.

We exited our vehicles at the same time. I itched to go to Lu, but couldn't leave Ricky to face the weres alone.

"They want a fight?" I asked.

"Neutral territory," Ricky reminded me, and I knew the werewolves were listening. "You took her." Summer pressed through the crowd, crossing the dry grass fast to stand in front of us. "You took Abbi into danger."

"Abbi wasn't taken from anyone," Ricky said. "She's

not owned by you. She's not a child. And how I hear it, she came to you asking for help to find her Shadow, and you kept her from doing that."

Ricky had always been warm with Lu, acting as a friend, a confidant. But in front of the gathered supernaturals, she was flint and steel, powder-dry and ready to catch.

"She was ours to protect," Summer said.

"She was ours," another voice chimed in, this one a man who was lean and muscled and golden brown in color. He faced off to her.

Summer tried to ignore him.

"She was all of ours," the man pressed. "You Riggs took her away—"

"—she came to us willingly—"

"—you promised you could find her Shadow. But you knew the Hush hunted. We told you they hunted. You knew the Hush thirsted for the Rabbit. You knew they would take her from us!"

"We were keeping her safe—"

He scoffed.

"—*safe*," she insisted. "And you were doing nothing for her, Cove."

Ricky whistled between her fingers, the sharp noise silencing them. "Shut up. Go home. Take your war off my land." She turned and opened her truck, reaching for Lu before I pushed Ricky to the side.

"I got her. You get the doors."

"Those ribs aren't gonna like that."

From the look I gave her, she knew exactly how much I cared about my ribs.

She left me to it, opening the door, which I followed her through.

My ribs hurt like hell, but Lu shifted slightly in my arms, turning her face into my chest, which sent a tremor of relief through me.

Ricky flicked lights on as she moved through the house. "She likes this room the most," she said. "I keep it for her."

Lu always stayed in this bedroom. It wasn't large, but was big enough for a queen-size bed with bright, mismatched pillows and quilts, and an iron headboard curled with flowers and leaves.

Unlike the other cluttered rooms, this was clean, smelling of fresh linen and the wild flowers in the vase on the dresser.

Ricky went around to the other side of the bed and turned the blankets down. I bent, easing Lu onto the mattress, holding my breath against the throbbing from my ribs, spine, and head.

"If I pushed you, you'd fall right in there beside her."

"Then don't push me."

"I'll get you some pain killers."

"I don't need them."

"You do. Lu might do her fastest healing sleeping, seeing she's not quite human, but you are turning several shades of green, blue, and black, my friend. I think your injuries might take longer to heal."

"Good thing someone here is suddenly an expert," I said.

Ricky chuckled. "I know, I know. There's never been

anything like you, hero. Back from the not-quite dead, and still not-quite alive.

"Nothing like Lu-lala either. I'm as game as you are to let you do this without blunting the pain. I'll, of course, take notes, so the next time you stumble into my house bleeding from a hundred bites and cuts, I can remind you that you're more interested in enduring discomfort than actually healing so you can be some use to Lu when she wakes up."

"Don't start making sense, Crossroads," I said, as I eased myself down into the wooden chair near the head of the bed. "It will destroy my opinion of you."

"I'll see if I have anything stronger than aspirin." She walked out of the room and closed the door halfway to give us a bit of privacy.

The sounds of voices outside rose and fell, but I tuned it out. This was neutral ground. If they really started a fight, Ricky could shut it down fast.

I smoothed Lu's hair off her forehead and rested my elbow on my thigh, head in my hand. I put my other hand over hers, closed my eyes, and tried to stay awake.

"…better if you just lie down. They want to have a conversation. It's going to take a while."

I lifted my head, which felt like it weighed a million pounds. "What?" I asked.

Val, looking faded and tired, leaned against the wall by the night stand. His wolf was barely an outline, sleeping, I thought, at his feet. Val waved to the glass of water and pills. "Pain killers. Ricky said they wouldn't knock you out, but since you were already asleep…" He shrugged.

I rolled my shoulders to try and get the kink out of my neck. Instead, I got a cramp under my shoulder blade.

"For fuck's sake," I growled.

"Water, pill. At least you have a way to dull the pain," Val said.

I fumbled with the pills, drank them down, finishing off the water in one go.

"What happened?" I asked.

"Out there? I don't know. The werewolves are arguing with Ricky about whether or not they're going back in after Abbi tonight."

I rubbed at my eyes. "Not that. With you and Lula in the cave."

"That was some amazing shit I did," he said with a wan smile. "You're welcome."

"You possessed my wife."

"I dove in there and went three rounds with the mother of all Hush. She was tying Lula up. She was going to kill her, Brogan."

I swallowed. "I know. I couldn't… I couldn't do anything. Couldn't move."

Val pointed at my mouth. "She did more than just bind your lips. She has her hooks in you."

"And Lu?"

He shook his head. "I cut through the ribbons she was spinning. I think just jumping into Lu cut most of the bindings."

"How did you get out? Away?"

He tipped his head to one side in question.

"We've… She's been possessed before," I told him.

"Ghosts. Usually they won't or can't leave. I have to drag them out of her. It's painful. For everyone."

"I woke up in this room," Val said. "I was in wolf form. Instinct is to get in the clear, get away from something that might harm me."

I looked down at Lu.

"She was unconscious when I fought Mother Hush," he said. "But I don't think she was injured. Not badly injured."

"And Abbi?"

"I searched before I found all of you pinned down. I couldn't find her."

"So are they going after her now?"

"No," Ricky said, coming through the door. "We'll wait until tonight."

"Because the dead of night worked so well last time," I said.

"No. Because it will give me time to make sure we are armed and properly protected. It will give the wolf packs time to prepare for battle, and," she added, "for you to sleep. We'll need you tonight, Brogan Gauge, even if Lu-lala hasn't recovered."

"Why? I was useless in there. What do you need me for?"

She nodded, her gaze on my lips and the Hush stitching there. "For bait."

S oft sheets, soft pillows, and Lula resting in my arms. I slept, waking only once when she gasped and softly called my name.

"I'm here," I said, pulling her closer, as her palm smoothed over my chest and her fingers gripped the cloth of my clean T-shirt. "We're out of the cave. We're safe at Ricky's."

I opened my eyes and looked down at her, but she was already asleep again, her breathing stronger than it had been, her grip on my shirt not loosening.

I thought of getting up, showering, eating something, but sleep took me down again.

The smell of warm apples and cinnamon woke me. I was alone in bed, but a cup of coffee and slice of hot apple cobbler steamed on the night stand.

I sat, breathing through the pain in my ribs. Lu's tinkling laughter drifted down the halls from the direction of the kitchen.

"She's cooking bacon." Val spooked in and sat on the bottom corner of the bed, staring out the half-open door. "I miss bacon."

Lu laughed again, this time a snorting chortle, and the sound of it made me relax. I picked up the coffee and took a drink, closing my eyes at the heat, the bitterness, the centering familiarity of the dark brew.

"I think they got a sniff of her baking. They're all coming back. So expect a crowd by the time you get down there."

"Who?" I tucked into the cobbler, shoveling in a huge bite and groaning in appreciation.

"Werewolves. A couple humans, too, if you can believe it. Ricky spent most of the morning talking to another Crossroads. She thinks she can better prepare us to get in and get Abbi out."

"And her Shadow," I said through a mouth of sticky, sweet, spicy dessert.

"Yeah, and her Shadow."

I gulped more coffee. "Why are you here?" I scraped the last of the filling onto the edge of my fork and licked it off.

"I'm delivering a message: Take a shower before coming down. Your clean clothes are on the chair." He pointed first at the hall, through which I knew was a bathroom, then at the chair where someone, probably Lu, had set out the denims and a T-shirt, socks, and a pair of boots with some miles on them but still in good shape.

Ricky's boots, if I had to guess.

I pushed back the covers, gathered the clothes, leaving the boots, and walked down to the bathroom.

"Why are you following me?" I asked Val.

"Are you worried I'm going to stare at your naked body?"

"Nope. I'm worried you're gonna complain non-stop while I'm trying to wash all the blood off.

He made a little considering sound. I walked into the bathroom and shut the door in his face, but he was dead, so he just walked right through the wall.

"Privacy would be nice."

"There are two people on this planet who can hear me. Ricky, who threatened to break our connection if I didn't shut up, and you."

"And Cupid." I threw the towel on the sink, stripped, and got into the shower.

"Who isn't here and doesn't really give a damn about me."

I poured shampoo into my palm and scrubbed it into my hair, then over my face and stubble. It smelled like limes and coconut.

"I've been thinking about the Hush," Val said.

I stuck my head under the water. The sloppy splat of soap hitting the drain didn't drown out Val's voice.

"Trying to figure out why they bound Rabbit's Shadow. What do they want with him? What are they doing with him?"

"Does it matter?" I asked.

"It should. I lost my life for it. You were injured. Lu was possessed. Why do they want Abbi?"

"She's an ancient spirit. Powerful."

"Why is Cupid looking for her?"

I grabbed the green bar of soap and scrubbed. "Do yourself a favor and don't try to understand the minds of gods."

"God of connections and destruction though, right? Bringing people together, tearing them apart?"

"Yep." I leaned a shoulder on the wall and scrubbed the bottom of my feet. "So?"

"Bo told you to do the right thing. That might mean taking Abbi to him."

I rotated under the spray, moving so it could loosen the knots in my back. "Maybe."

"Turning her over to a god might not be a good

idea. I've heard, well, it's been said for a long time, that the gods are at war."

"Yep. Powerful beings can't help but spit on each other's shoes."

"Is Abbi a pawn in that? Gods spitting on gods?"

"There hasn't been another god looking for her. Not even one of the moon goddesses. If she's a pawn, no one's claiming her. I think Abbi can make her own choices when we get her back."

"Have you read the legends about the Moon Rabbit?"

"Have you?"

"Just this morning. In one of them she pounds a pestle and mortar. You know what some legends say she's making?"

"Moon cakes?"

"Yeah, some say that. Some say medicine for mortals."

I turned off the taps and shoved aside the shower curtain. "All right."

"Other tales say she's making the elixir of life. For immortals."

It might have just been the drafty old house, but goosebumps prickled across my skin. "Huh."

"I'm thinking the Hush…you saw them. Do you think they'd want that? The elixir of life?"

"Mother Hush didn't want Abbi," I said. "She wants…" I tried to say the book, the Strange weave, but the words locked in my throat. I broke out in an instant sweat.

"The book. I know. I heard her. You don't have to say it."

I focused on breathing. When I could move, I picked up the towel and dried off. "I don't think the two things, Abbi and…"

"…the god's spell book," he supplied.

"…have anything to do with each other."

Valentine messed with the leather lacings on his wrist, fingering the beads like he was working an abacus. "They took her Shadow. When he was falling. They wanted Abbi enough to take him. Trap him."

I dressed, thinking it over. Why did Cupid want us to find Abbi and *do the right thing*? Was he worried she'd fall into the hands of the Hush? Or did he want us to find out what the Hush were doing? Did he want to know what move they were going to play in finding the book?

Were we all just pawns in a god war?

"He said I'd know the Rabbit when we found her," Val said. "I did know her and her Shadow too. But is that all I was supposed to do? Was that all I was good for?"

"You're good for annoying me," I said.

His expression, which had looked pretty lost, fell into a familiar scowl.

"I'm good for a hell of a lot more than that."

"Tell Bo that when we see him again. Until then, you'll just have to help us save Abbi and her Shadow from the Hush."

"What happens if we get her out of there?"

"*When* we get her out of there, we'll do the right thing by letting her choose her own the next step."

Val's grin was swift and sharp, and it put a spark in his eyes I hadn't seen. "You'd go against a god and let the Rabbit run away?"

"Gods and I have never much seen eye-to-eye." I strode into the bedroom, put on soft socks and the boots, which fit perfectly, then headed down the hall. Val was already in the kitchen by the time I got there.

And so were fifty other people.

Werewolves chatted and laughed and grumbled as they gave each other no space but plenty of side-eye. Most of them were spooning apple compote over waffles and eating them as quickly as Lu and Ricky could get them out of the iron.

I knew they'd heard me coming, because I wasn't trying to be quiet, and they were werewolves, but only two looked up as I strode into the kitchen: Summer and Cove, who I thought was the leader of the Kearney pack.

I met both of their gazes, and for a moment, I was angry at them. For how they'd failed Abbi, yes, but also how they hadn't protected one of their own: Valentine.

Val stood apart from all of the others, the look on his face a mix of sorrow and anger and longing.

Danube was searching the room. His gaze stalled on the corner where Val sulked. I thought he was going to wend his way through the crowd, but Ricky was there, bending close to Val and saying something that drew Valentine out of his slouch, and put that sharp smile back on his face.

When Ricky pulled away, she threw a look at Danube, then went back to helping Lu with the waffles.

Val had disappeared, but I figured he wasn't far off.

Lu turned toward me and winked, and there was nothing that could keep me from her. The werewolves shifted out of my way, as if they knew the only thing for me in that kitchen was a red-headed woman with a ladle in her hand.

She watched me walk her way, taking in my face, my chest, the right side of my torso—where my ribs still twinged if I breathed wrong—and my scuffed knuckles.

I'd seen the bruises on my face, and while they didn't look great, they'd already faded from black to a muddy green.

"Breakfast smells good," I said, crowding in on her.

"You play your cards right, and I'll give you the next waffle fresh off the iron."

"Don't want a waffle." I lifted the ladle out of her hand and tugged her toward me.

"Breakfast—"

"Time for a coffee break. Have you eaten?"

"She has not." Ricky handed me a plate with waffle, apple compote, syrup, and a large mug of black coffee. "Table on the porch is free."

"I'm not finished with the cooking," Lu protested, but she stole the coffee and took a big gulp.

"It will be here when you get back." I guided her out of the kitchen.

This time every person in the room wanted to say a thank you, or comment on how delicious the food was. It was taking us so long to cross the room, I could feel a growl building in my chest.

The hall had more people in it now, and a steady

stream of folks were coming through the door, following their noses to Lu's amazing cooking, just like Val had said.

We finally broke through to the porch overlooking the back of the lot. The porch was quiet, mostly empty, and Lorde was sprawled out in the grass, soaking up the early morning sunlight.

Even though the building was on the intersection of two roads, hardly anyone ever drove this way. That meant the sound of birds and bugs was loud, as were the voices of werewolves, coming toward the house.

I spotted the little round table Ricky had placed in the corner, put Lu's plate there, then carted a second chair over so I could sit beside her, both of us looking out at the grass and our dog.

Lorde just glanced over at us and yawned, showing off her black tongue, then put her head down on her paws.

"I'm fine," Lu said, picking up the fork and cutting a square of waffle." She pointed it at me, apple and maple dripping. "You didn't have to push me out here." She ate that bite and immediately took another.

I waited until she stopped demolishing the waffle long enough to take a sip of coffee. "You haven't eaten for too long. And you used up resources healing. Do you need something else, Lu?"

She knew what I was asking: Did she need blood? She wasn't a vampire, and didn't need blood to survive. She had only drunk a handful of times since we'd been attacked, when it had been the only way her body could heal, the only way she could survive.

She sipped her coffee. "No. I'm good. Though I should probably eat something that isn't mostly sugar."

"I think Ricky has hummus and spinach in there."

She crinkled her nose. "Later." She cut another large wedge of waffle and stuffed it in her mouth.

"I couldn't stop her," I said. "Mother Hush. I was frozen. But I saw… I saw what she did to you."

Lu caught my hand in hers. "I didn't keep you safe either." She waved her fork in a circle, indicating the bruises still visible on my face.

"Bruises heal," I grumbled.

"I know. But when I saw you frozen, all those bruises and the blood…" She slipped her hand into mine. "I can't see you that way, Brogan. I…" She shook her head, her lips pressed together. "I want you to stay behind."

"No."

"I see how the world treats you. Coming back alive has been like throwing yourself into a rock tumbler. Facing down that evil in the caverns isn't a part of your job description. It's not your fight."

"No? You think I should leave Abbi down there, when I was the one who lost her?"

Lu's nostrils flared. I knew she wanted to yell at me. In a way, I'd welcome it.

She'd been treating me with kid gloves. I had enough self-awareness to know I'd been doing the same to her.

Worse, I hadn't asked her for help when I was struggling.

"You're right," I said to stave off the fight and to

own up to my part. "I'm… It hasn't been easy. Living. The world. It's hard, Lu. Sometimes it's too much."

Her glare shifted into something awfully close to panic, and I squeezed her hand. "I'm figuring it out. Working on getting more used to…everything. Getting used to the rock tumbler. I thought I was hiding it pretty well."

"I've known you for nearly a century, Brogan."

I tipped my head down just a little, catching her gaze. "You don't want my help either, Lula. Think back on it. Gas stations, the flat tire, the hotel you wouldn't agree to. Those nights you refused to sleep because you were afraid I'd disappear in the night. I saw the tears on your cheeks in the morning, love, even though you said everything was fine."

She leaned back in her chair, looking away across the yard. Her cheeks warmed with pink.

"I don't always do that," she said.

"I know."

"What would it matter if I told you I was afraid? Why should you stay up all night facing down my fears?"

"Because I love you. Because I want to face everything right beside you. Even if it's fear. Especially if it's fear."

She closed her eyes, and I contented myself with the sensation of her hand, warm in mine, the soft rhythm of her breaths, her perfume mixed with apple waffles and maple.

"You're not going to stay here at Ricky's while we go back to the caverns are you?" she asked.

"Are you?"

"No."

"Then no."

"If I were?"

"I'd still have to go. I know she's not a child, but… I hate to think of her facing the Hush on her own."

She was quiet, her eyes still closed.

"I'm sorry, Lu."

Her eyes opened, and I was caught in the honey light. "For?"

"You are stuck with me."

A small smile brushed her lips. "Since it's my dream come true, I think I can stand it."

The crunch of tires on gravel caught the attention of the four werewolves chatting out near the trees. Lorde faced the approaching car, her tail curled and stiff.

Ricky stepped out of the house, glanced at us, then leaned on the post at the top of the steps just like she had when we'd arrived. At that casual contact of her shoulder to the post, the entire house rang softly, the sound in the center of my chest like a harp string struck by a hammer.

The magic steeped into the walls of this house, echoed in Ricky. I could feel wards snap into place, sharp like mint hard candy, could feel the sweet bay aftershocks of magic waking.

"You know them?" I asked Ricky.

"Nope. You?"

I couldn't see through the windshield, but I knew I'd seen that car somewhere before. "Not sure."

"The thrift shop," Lu said. "Mr. Walch. The man from the thrift shop."

Sure enough, the car came to a stop on the driveway, and out of it stepped Mr. Walch. He glared at all of us on the porch, then trundled around the car to the trunk.

The passenger side door opened, and the mother I'd seen in the shop got out and shut the door behind her. "Are you Ricky, um, the Crossroads?" she asked.

Lorde had moved closer to us, keeping between us and the car. Her tail wagged uncertainly.

"I'm Ricky," she said. "This is the Crossroads."

Which, well, wasn't exactly a lie. But it wasn't just this place that was a Crossroad, *she* was the Crossroads where magic, and information, and creatures came to sort things out.

Where we'd come to sort things out too.

"*You're* the Crossroads, right? Because that's who we're looking for."

"And you are?"

"Right. Sorry. I'm Pamela Walch. This is my grandfather, Elmer Walch. We're here to hunt the Hush."

She pulled a necklace out from under her blue and white polka-dotted sweater, and I stiffened.

Hunters—monster hunters—were a loosely connected group of people who liked to put stakes in people like me.

That necklace stank of the hunter mark. It was everything I could do not to put myself in front of Lu and tell her to run.

"Hunter," Ricky said smoothly, her voice a little deeper as she sucked in the magic of the house.

I thought, for a moment, every blade of grass shimmered gold. I thought, for a moment, the air shivered silver.

I thought, for a moment, Ricky would snap her fingers, and Pamela would evaporate on the spot.

"I don't think you want to be here today," Ricky said.

"We're going to go find that girl tonight, right? Abbi?"

Ricky shrugged and lines of magic shimmered out from where she stood, traveling under the grass in colors I could barely sense, wrapping around Pamela's feet.

If she felt the magic, Pamela didn't show it.

The magic continued around to Elmer who was complaining under his breath while dragging a wooden box out of the trunk.

The magic pooled around his feet, and Elmer's head came up. "Keep your slabber of gee haw magic off me, Crossroads. We are what we are. Right here in plain sight. We know you got werewolves roaming around."

"Hunters don't take kindly to werewolves," Ricky said.

"Yeah, yeah. But this here is neutral ground. Finding that little girl is more important than making the Riggs' or Kearneys' lives messy." He went back to shoving things around in the trunk. "Got enough mess, don't I? Son-in-law went off and became the sheriff, damn fool."

Ricky shifted her shoulder away from the column.

"Perfectly good store he coulda run. Except for all the werewolves scaring off business."

Pamela rolled her eyes. "I've told you a million

times. They don't have anything to do with how many people stop in your shop, Gramps. You need to advertise. Some flyers, a web page. Something."

"When you take over the shop, you can advertise." He shuffled past her with a heavy crate in his arms. The crate was full of Mason jars, small ones that held things like jam, and they jangled as he set the crate on the bottom step.

"There you go," he said. "All the Rooroo dust I could get on short notice. I expect to be informed the next time we poke the Hush in their holes, Crossroads." He stomped up the stairs and past all three of us. "Is that waffles I smell? Hey, Rigg! Dish me up a three stack. I do my best rescuing on a full belly."

I expected to hear snarling, arguing, some kind of push back. But someone said something, and half the place started chuckling.

"He's got a big mouth," Pamela said, "but a bigger heart. He told me Abbi was missing. From how worried all the wolves were, we figured it was supernatural. The Hush?"

"The Hush," Ricky agreed. "Do you know what Abbi is?"

"Moon Rabbit, right?"

Ricky nodded.

Pamela grinned, and I could see the freckle-faced child she'd once been. "Gramps thought she was a moon goddess, but I was pretty sure she was the Rabbit. Just won me a dinner at Applebee's."

"What's in the jars?" Lu asked.

Pamela started forward. "Rooroo dust. It's a family

recipe. Works on the Hush like salt on ghosts or holy water against demons. Throw a little on them, and they'll freeze and burn."

"You've tried it?" Lu asked.

"All us Walch kids keep some near our beds. Ever since—according to family lore—our aunt was stolen out of her cradle and possessed by one of the Hush.

"She and the Hush fought, seeing as Aunty didn't like sharing her brain with any other creature. She rolled around in Rooroo dust, and the Hush took off in a shot. But then she got lonely and spent a couple decades going from cave to cave apologizing and hoping to see the Hush again."

Ricky chuckled. "I've heard of her. She married the Hush, didn't she? Your aunt was Old Ruby?"

"The same."

"Raised that Hush kid for a while, right?"

"Yeah, but Thrum disappeared the day she died. Went back in the caves, they say."

I stilled. I knew that name. My dream?

"Auntie's welcoming approach to the supernatural sort of runs in the family," Pamela said.

"We've got no beef with the weres," she added. "Well, Gramps thinks they're running people off his shop, but if he used a broom more than once a year, I think a lot more people would show up."

Pamela extended her hand to Lu.

Lu crossed her arms over her chest.

Pam stuck her hand in her pocket, not seeming concerned that Lu had refused the handshake.

"Since it might need saying: I have no quarrel with

the weres, the Rabbit, Crossroads, or the two of you—
whatever you may be. I do want to make sure the Hush
aren't stepping out of line, stealing people and such. Just
like my family's been making sure for centuries."

"You do that, we'll have no troubles," Lu said
evenly.

Pamela must have caught the warning in Lu's tone,
because she took a step closer to Ricky. "I'd be happy to
pay for Gramps' meal. Mine too, if you have extra."

"We have plenty," Summer said from the door.
"Come on in Pam. I brewed tea."

"Hey, Sum." Pamela strode past Ricky and followed
the head of the Riggs pack. "You know I would have
helped if I knew you were going up against the Hush."

"It's not something we planned," Summer replied,
her voice fading as she strolled deeper into the house.
"Abbi ran off. Things went downhill from there."

"You trust her?" Lu asked Ricky.

"I don't know her," she said. "But if she wanted to
cause problems, she would have taken her shot when
they first drove up. I'd know if she were lying."

"The magic you sent out to her?" I asked.

She raised her dark eyebrows. "Magic?"

"You pulled it out of the house and sent it through
the grass."

"You saw that?"

I shrugged.

"What else do you see, Brogan Gauge?" For a
moment, Ricky was more. Her eyes burned lavender
with power, her body built of stone and iron, wings

curving above her head. The tattoos became a living river of symbols, motion and magic, ancient as the stars.

"I see that you have a house full of trouble," I said. "The minute they're off your property, all hell's going to break loose."

Ricky sucked air through her teeth, and she was suddenly herself again. A smug smile on her face. "I spent some time consulting with another Crossroads this morning."

"Which one?" Lu asked.

She winced. "Nick."

"You talked to your dad?" Lu said.

Ricky leaned over the porch rail and spit down into the grass. "I can deal with assholes if they give me the answers I need."

"Did he?" I asked.

She nodded. "Eventually."

"So," I said, "you have a plan for how to keep the werewolves, hunters, and the rest of us from killing each other as soon as we're clear of neutral ground?"

"I do."

"Does it involve magic?" Lu asked.

She bent at the waist, a bit of a bow, a bit of a performance. "Of course it does, my Lu-lala. All the best things do."

CHAPTER FIFTEEN

It took most of the day to pull everything together. The wolves got into a few arguments, but weirdly, let themselves be shouted down by Elmer, who called them all dumbasses and reminded them they were on the same side, trying to rescue the Moon Rabbit.

It was also Elmer who first rolled up his sleeve to let Ricky mark him with magic.

"How long is it gonna last?" Elmer asked.

We'd all moved out into the great room, werewolves sprawled on the couches, the floor, leaning on the walls, perched on the deep windowsills. Pamela had taken up the assistant position, helping Ricky spread out artist brushes, pens, and inkwells she'd retrieved from one of the many rooms.

Lu and I were closest to the doorway, her hip leaned back against mine, my arms dropped around her, fingers hooked into her belt loop. It positioned us the farthest from the hunters, something we'd done on purpose.

"Should last until dawn. Maybe a little less," Ricky

said. "Depends on the group and how much strain is put on the bindings."

"Wait." Elmer pulled his arm away from Ricky's brush. "Talk me through it."

"This," Ricky held a delicate brush in her big mitt, an inkwell in the other, "is the magic of this neutral ground. Once you all carry my mark," she wiggled the paintbrush, "we will be connected, all of us to each other, through me, through this land. It might be uncomfortable at first."

"Pain?" Elmer sniffed. "I'm not afraid of pain."

"No, it's not that kind of pain," Ricky said. "Some of you might feel other people's feelings or moods much more strongly than you'd like. Sometimes—it's rare, but sometimes—thoughts will spike through the connections, and you'll know what someone is thinking…or what several dozen people are thinking."

"We have pack bonds," Danube noted. "We're already connected."

"We don't need it," a dark-haired Kearney woman agreed.

There was a rise and fall of agreement.

"This is deeper than pack bonds," Ricky said. "Do I need to remind you that we are not all in the same pack?"

Several of the wolves snorted and snarled at the idea of being tied to another pack.

Ricky shrugged. "I'm not asking you to like it. I'm just telling you the Hush know your connections. They know how to smother them. They know how to confuse you and lead you into danger.

"My magic is built out of things the Hush can't touch, can't control, can't break. You're going into their territory. Their nest. They have all the advantage. This is the best way, the only way I know how, to give you an upper hand."

"Well, that and Rooroo dust," Elmer said. "I suppose we can scrub the mark off as soon as the rescue's done?"

"I can cancel it. It will wear off in just a few hours, maybe faster for the humans since you aren't natural to this kind of thing. A little slower for werewolves who have this awareness built into their DNA."

"What about them?" Danube thumbed toward Lu and me.

All the faces turned to study us, many of them curious, more than one person sniffing the air as if still trying to decide what sort of creatures we were.

"They know you're different," Valentine said.

Danube's gaze tacked where the ghost had appeared on the other side of Lu, half standing in the bookshelf.

Ricky opened the inkwell and dipped the brush.

"Like I said," she replied, "it will connect all of us. Even Lu and Brogan. I'm hoping for a solid four hours. From this moment forward. Let's do this quickly."

She dipped the brush into the well, and a glowing line of magic pulled out with the brush. She flicked her wrist and, with three quick strokes, transferred the magic to Elmer's forearm.

The magic flared purple, softened to a sunset hue, and then there was nothing but the faintest glow on his skin.

"That it?" Elmer asked.

"That's it." Ricky turned to the room, and I could see the echo of light in her eyes, a slight hint of madness swimming there. I wondered what it would cost her to be the center point for all these connections, but then she smiled, and the madness, the magic in her eyes was gone. "Lu-lala?"

She stepped forward, and I let my fingers fall from her belt loop, following her, step-for-step to Ricky.

Lula held out the back of her hand, and I did the same, our hands leveled to create a single canvas. Ricky made a considering noise, dipped the brush, and began.

It took a few more strokes to paint the mark on us, but Ricky had a deft touch. The magic poured into my skin and sent a taste that was warm like wintergreen and soft like caramel rolling through my senses.

Lu leaned into me a little closer, I did the same with her, and when Ricky lifted the brush from Lu's skin, there was a visible snap, like an electrical current had tripped.

"Is that supposed to…" I started to ask. But then I could feel Elmer connected to me in a way only one person ever had been.

He wasn't unpleasant, like a wool flannel shirt that was a little too large wasn't unpleasant, but I not only felt him, I could feel what he was feeling.

Elmer felt the connection to Ricky—a muffled experience for Elmer that came roaring at me like an ocean wave of power and force.

Elmer felt his connection to me, and that echoed

back at me like death, like destruction, like connections broken and bleeding.

Elmer felt Lu, burning bright, a nearly painful flame.

All of it doubled for me. It was a lot. It was too much. I inhaled, held it.

Lu squeezed my hand, her flame spread out like a wing, shielding me from the sensations, the connections.

"I just need some air," I said, faintly.

Lu guided me out of the room. I knew the moment the first werewolf was marked, because I could feel her doubt and her surprise.

"She said she can break it," Lu said, and I realized I was sitting at the table on the porch again, her hand rubbing small circles between my shoulder blades.

"She also said it wears off. Four hours." I took a good breath and let it out, settling myself with the ever-growing noise of other people building in my mind, Lu's touch grounding me like nothing else could.

"You don't have to do this," she said softly. "You could stay with Lorde."

I sat back and gazed up at her. "Not a single fucking chance." I smiled to take the heat out of my words.

"You know there's stubborn, and then there's stupid," she observed.

"And then there's the perfect blend of both." I stood, caught her face between my palms, and gently tipped it up toward me. She went with the motion willingly.

"I am the perfect blend," I noted in case she wasn't following along. Then I kissed the smirk off her face.

· · ·

I wasn't the only one who chafed under the magic. Several of the weres hated it enough they had Ricky remove it.

They'd been told they were not allowed on the rescue mission without the mark. Both packs enforced the rule. The weres grumbled, but agreed.

Pamela's girlfriend, Josie, met us alongside the road, near the cavern, bringing an amazing artillery of weapons, ropes, and lights.

For a hunter, Josie was quick to smile, quick to give the werewolves shit. She was also quick to back up Pamela who was currently telling one of the werewolves that none of the hunters could hurt them without every single wolf knowing they were going to try it before they actually tried it.

The weres might not trust the hunters, and the hunters might not trust Lu and me, but Ricky's connection leveled the ground.

I was reasonably sure no one would turn the rescue mission into a killing spree.

"You must be Brogan," Josie said before slapping a salt shaker full of Rooroo dust into my hand. "Pamela said you're not were. Any chance you'll tell me what you are?" She batted her thick eyelashes, really laying on the fake charm, the warm rose undertones in her dark skin making her soft hazel eyes pop.

"Doesn't seem likely," I said.

"Had to try." She handed a shaker of dust to Lu. "You just don't…" She shook her head. "Sorry, it's rude."

"I can handle rude," I said, curious.

"Neither of you make sense to me." She tapped her forehead. "To my sight. Sometimes you don't look alive, and other times, you're both wrapped in so much power, glory, I wonder if you're a couple gods playing us dirty."

We hadn't run into a Sighted—someone who could see the supernatural truth of someone—for decades.

"We're not gods," Lu said. "If we were, we wouldn't have lost Abbi."

Josie nodded, but made a sound like that still wasn't enough to convince her. "What about the ghost?"

Val was currently leaning on the bumper of Silver, bitching at both wolf packs.

"What about him?" I asked.

"Well, is he with you? Because if not…" She opened her flannel shirt to reveal another small shaker filled with what looked like salt.

"He's with us," Lu said.

"We wouldn't take kindly to you banishing him," I added, which earned me a strange look from Lu. "What?" I asked. "He's a part of this. A part of saving Abbi, of doing the 'right thing.' Just because he annoys the crap out of me doesn't mean I want to see him banished."

"Aw," Lu said, taking my hand and making big eyes at me. "You like him."

"I do not."

"A little," she insisted.

"Not even. I barely tolerate him."

"He is the first ghost friend you've made. I'm so proud of you."

"Nope. That's the end of that. I'll just go throw myself down a hole so I don't have to listen to this nonsense."

Lu, chuckling, grabbed at my sleeve as I faked my anger and started to storm off.

"Settle down. It's fine, it's fine," she laughed. "I take it back. You have no friends and never will."

"What did you just say?" I wasn't as incensed as I sounded, but she had caught me off guard. Her laughter snagged me even as I realized the accusation wasn't that far from the truth. "I have friends."

"Oh?" She moved in closer, a predator ready to pounce. "Who are your friends, Brogan Gauge?" She wrapped her hands around me, sticking slim fingers just beneath the edge of my belt.

"You," I said, breathy and hypnotized.

"No, I'm more than that. Who's just a friend of yours?"

"Lorde."

"Lorde is a dog."

"Man's best friend."

"Valentine," Lu said.

"I've heard of him."

"He could be your friend. I think he wants to be."

"I don't like ghosts." I wanted to capture the light flowing through her, the joy she was finding in just this moment, in an argument that I didn't care if I won or lost.

"Ricky is your friend," she said.

"No, she's not."

"She certainly the hell is," Ricky said, breaking the moment.

I scowled at her. Most of the werewolves were watching Lu and I with heads tipped, like we were a double feature with free popcorn refill.

"Private conversation," I growled. A wave of amusement rolled through the connections.

"Wrong time for privacy," Ricky noted, "and wrong time for conversation. We need to hit while the magic's hot. You have your weapons?"

Lu and I nodded. We hadn't escaped the last trip into the caverns with the weapons she had given us, but Ricky had produced two more. For Lu, another dagger, for me, another lightning rod. Both a little different, but still wielding magic that should stop the Hush.

"You're not going in with us are you, Ricky?" Lu asked.

"I'll stay out here. The connections…" Her eyes flashed lavender, before going back to a warm brown. "…they are a lot for me to hold. Especially this far away from my house."

"You don't have to carry all of us," Lu said. "Brogan and I—"

"It's all or nothing, Lu-lala. Against the Hush that even the Moon Rabbit couldn't escape? We stick together. Don't worry," she added with a grin. "I only plan on doing it once. So you'd better bring Abbi and Hado out of there."

"Good thing we have such a bullet-proof plan," I said.

Our plan had two steps. One: Find Abbi and her Shadow. Two: get out alive.

The sun sank toward the horizon, slow and warm as molasses. It wouldn't be fully dark for at least two hours, but our connections wouldn't last for much longer than that.

Now was the time to enter the cave. Now was the time to save Abbi.

I pulled Lu closer, threading my fingers up along her cheek and into the wild autumn of her hair. She came to me until we stood, forehead to forehead.

"I love you," I said.

"I love you," she replied.

Her words settled in me, and the roaring wave of noise, feelings, sensations bombarding me through the connections, eased.

Summer spoke in a low voice. "We go in packs of three. Riggs will take all the right branching tunnels, Kearneys, left."

"Threes for us too," Cove said. "Left tunnels. Anyone is hurt, someone helps them find the way out. No one goes alone."

"Follow this." Ricky gave a little tug on the connections. They flared bright, hot, and burned a clear path to her.

There was no way any of us would miss seeing or feeling that, no matter how deep or twisted the path became.

"Can everyone feel that?" she asked.

The weres made affirmative noises, and Elmer, Pamela, and Josie all said yes.

"Brogan, Lula?" she asked.

"We felt it," Lula said.

"Good hunting to you, friends," Ricky said.

Her heart, Lu's heart, and all the others, beat faster, eager for the hunt. That energy zinged through all of us, building.

"Brogan doesn't have friends," Danube said. "So I hear."

A few of the weres still in human form chuckled.

"I'll be your friend," Danube said, as he strode past us.

"I'll be your friend too," Josie said.

"I don't want anything to do with you," Elmer said.

Pamela laughed and shoved her grandfather forward.

Val came up beside me.

"Don't say it," I said to him.

"Well, I was going to say I already am your friend, but now that Danube likes you, I'm rethinking our entire relationship."

"We don't have a relationship."

"I'm practically a brother to you."

"No."

The handful of the weres in human form stripped out of their clothing and shifted into wolf.

"Good thing we aren't alongside a road," I muttered. "Good thing we aren't out in the open, in broad daylight or anything."

Lu huffed a laugh, as we strode across the road, a flow of wolves streaming ahead of us, around us, and still more behind us.

"I saved Lula," Val said.

I finally looked over at him. He was floating along, matching our speed, a determined look on his face. He looked at me. "I did."

"I know. I didn't thank you."

A small smile hooked his lips. "No, you did not."

"Thank you."

"You are welcome. I like her very much. And I have a rather unhealthy hatred of the Hush. I couldn't, and would never, let them hurt her."

"Neither would I. I'm glad you were there for her."

"Thanks for telling the hunters not to banish me." He cupped his hand on one side of his mouth, like anyone other than Ricky and I could hear him, and fake whispered: "That salt won't banish me."

"How do you know?"

"I was haunting a hole-in-the-wall bar, Brogan. A lot of salt gets spilled in places like that."

I laughed, which only encouraged him.

"Pretzels get thrown at people on the regular. Salted peanuts too. Don't even get me started on the one-dollar margarita night. No ghost with any brains would stay in that kind of hostile environment if salt bothered them."

"Val say something?" Lu asked.

"He fought the Hush for you."

"I know. I thanked him for that. I told him I owe him a favor."

I stopped, and it took Lu three more steps before she looked back. "What?"

"You know he'll just hang around waiting to collect."

And oh, how she smiled. "I happen to enjoy the company of incorporeal men."

I scowled, and she widened her eyes in mock innocence.

"*One* incorporeal man," I said. "You enjoy the company of one." I pointed at my chest, and then she was there, in my space, her hand over my heart.

"You're not incorporeal now," she said. "You are solid. Alive." I heard the words, and I heard what was behind them. She was claiming me. Claiming her right to this life we had fought so hard for. The realness of it. The togetherness.

"I'm not going to leave you, Lu. Not ever."

She tipped her chin in just the slightest of nods.

"Val said he's not afraid of salt," I said, changing the subject.

"Josie's going to be disappointed," she said.

"Josie ain't got no time for ghosts," Josie called from ahead of us. Then, within a few more steps, we all fell silent.

We were at the cavern opening. This was the breath before we stepped off the edge of the world, the airlock before we threw ourselves into the void. This was our last second of sunlight, of green.

Our bonds glowed with power, gold as sunlight, strong as hope, burning with violet fury. There was moonlight in it, too—our fondness for Abbi, who had, in her own way, tied us together. The little rabbit from the moon, who we would not leave behind, alone in the dark.

Summer's back was to the cave entrance, Cove stood next to her.

Summer crossed her fingers and held it over her heart. Maybe for luck. Maybe the sign language sign for the letter "R" for Riggs. The Riggs still in human form made the sign back to her.

Cove threw his own gesture, dragging his thumb across his forehead, back to his temple. The Kearney's echoed the sign.

Silent as hope, the werewolves slipped into darkness.

CHAPTER SIXTEEN

Elmer adjusted the sling on the shotgun he'd insisted on bringing. "Go on," he said, as Lu and I passed. "We're with you."

He clapped me on the shoulder. His hand was warm and strong. The assurance in his eyes was that of a hunter who had waded into the nests of too many strange creatures to count.

A hunter who had gotten out alive. He seemed younger, suddenly stronger. I could see the hunter he had been over the years: smart, solid, steady.

I was glad he was on our side.

I took a step, but Lu was quicker and slipped in front of me. I would argue, but it would be out of pride more than sense. Lu could fight the Hush as well, or frankly, better than me. Her reflexes were faster, her strength possibly greater than mine.

She had spent nearly a hundred years hunting and fighting dangerous things.

"Don't get distracted," Val said from next to me,

which should be impossible in the narrow tunnel, except he was a ghost and could pass through rock. "Pay attention."

I didn't waste my breath telling him I was plenty aware of the stink of damp, of the dust, and the uneven rise and fall of the stone beneath my soles.

I didn't tell him every connection flashed through my mind, so I felt like I was dozens of people, dozens of feet, hands, eyes.

Panic, maybe mine, maybe ours, stirred my gut.

This darkness was where I'd lost Abbi. This darkness was where I'd almost lost Lu. This darkness was where the Hush had dragged my sleeping mind to stitch my mouth closed. To force me to bow to their demands.

To find the book, the Strange weave, and bring it to them.

"Got your back," Val whispered.

It helped, knowing he was there. "Still not my friend," I managed, and was relieved when he chuckled.

"This way," Lu reached back, her hand finding mine.

This was where the tunnel diverged. I felt connections spool off to the right, like a dozen kite strings pulling taut on a choppy breeze, and then another set of strings unraveled to the left.

Lu continued forward. I could hear Elmer's strides behind me, but the stone and darkness muffled Pamela and Josie, just behind him.

The hint of the hunters' red flashlights reminded me that Josie had given me a flashlight.

I dug it out of my pocket, leaving the bottle of

Rooroo dust behind, clicked the light, and exhaled when it cast ruby light over stone.

Lu turned sideways through a tight space, and I did the same. Cold stone scratched at my chest and belly. I blew out a breath and pressed through the narrow passage.

The other side of that tight space opened into branching paths. We had two choices.

Lu tipped her head, and Val spooked by me, splitting into two, man and wolf, each moving quickly down the paths ahead of us.

"Val," I whispered to Lu. She nodded.

Val and his wolf returned together from the right path.

"This way."

We followed the tunnel to the right, which slanted at a hard angle downward. I braced my descent with one hand pressed against the wall, the other holding the flashlight.

Someone, maybe Pamela, cursed behind me, her flashlight swinging sharply before steadying.

The footing grew more treacherous. Lu moved nimbly and quickly ahead of me, ducking when the ceiling lowered, staying on her feet over the slippery rubble.

"Here, here," Val whispered. "Right up here."

Then there was darkness, snuffing all light. I took a blind step and was pulled back, hard. A hand clamped over my mouth, another around my neck. I hit something solid behind me—*too soft to be stone, but only barely*—something familiar.

"Be silent," the male voice said. The same voice from my dream that had guided me out of the caverns. Thrum.

"We know what you seek. We know who you are. But you are marked, *two-soul*. You must stay while they go."

My heart hammered so loudly I was amazed it wasn't echoing back from the walls.

The red lights had stopped moving. Each person in our group had been hauled to the side by a Hush.

"We will lead them to where she is hidden. Where they are both hidden," Thrum said. "But you must remain."

It was a trick. It had to be a trick. But then Lu was in front of me, her eyes narrowed, her teeth bared, weapon raised.

"Let him go," she snarled.

Thrum released me and somehow *flowed* out from behind me, reforming just out of Lu's reach. Another Hush, who had been behind Lu formed next to him.

"We will lead you to the Rabbit and Shadow. But he must stay," Thrum said. "Mother Hush will know if he enters the chamber. He bears her mark."

"Let them all go," Lu demanded.

The Hush released Pamela, Elmer, and Josie. The hunters backed up to us, weapons raised.

"We will help you find them," Thrum said. "We will take you to them."

"Why should we believe you?" I asked.

"If they try anything, I'll kill them." Val and his wolf

appeared next to Lu, the wolf growling, Val looking like vengeance unleashed.

The Hush moved backward, away from him.

"What?" Lu asked.

"Val," I said.

"Mother Hush's mistake was killing me the first time," Val said. "I know her now. I know how to destroy her, and I know how to destroy you."

Thrum was the only Hush who stepped forward to face him. "Tell them to follow us. We will take you to the Moon and Shadow."

Lu caught my eyes in the low light. "Yes?" she asked.

"Val?" I asked.

"Tell her yes, Brogan," he said. "Abbi's down there."

"Val says she's down there," I said. "He also said he'll kill the Hush if they lead us into a trap."

"It *is* a trap," Thrum said with what sounded like exasperation. "But if we are quick, we may escape before it's sprung. You should stay here," he said to me.

"No," Lu said again. "We don't separate."

Thrum tipped his head and made a sound that might have been a sigh. "More important for her to be taken from here. If you insist on risking him, come."

He stepped past Lu and pressed something on the right side of the steep tunnel. The stones opened to reveal a wide tunnel. Lichen glowed a delicate blue from floor to ceiling in beautiful lacework patterns.

"Maybe I should stay," I said to Lu.

"No." The one word was fierce. "I'm not losing you."

Lu moved, swiftly following the Hush into the indigo-blue light.

I glanced at Val. "Stay with us. With her."

"I know." He split again, his wolf leaping away from him and moving to the back of our group, while the human shape of him ghosted ahead, catching up with Lu.

I jogged after them, Elmer muttering and cursing about the damned shady Hush were not to be trusted, and that you *never* split up the group in caverns where it would be too damn easy to get so lost you died.

Here, the air was warmer, scented with strange flowers, with honey and pine.

Here, the dust kicked up, motes sparkling blue before falling back to the ancient stone.

Here, I could feel the gazes of creatures even older than the Hush, spirits of the mountains, the underworld.

Did the dark gods watch our progress? Did any god?

That, I was sure, didn't matter. All we could do was follow our instincts, our hearts. All we could do was hold each other through the darkness, doing what we could, doing the hard thing to keep the vulnerable safe. To find a child who was not a child, and her Shadow who was not a shadow, and return them to the sky.

Time slid by in all the shades of blue. I was still too new to the living world to intuit time, but this felt endless. There was nothing but our swift steps down a twisted path, each breath stretching out, dreamlike.

And then—

—*a crack of thunder*—

—the tunnel opened into a magic-drenched chamber—

—*light flared, died*—

—and Abbi stood up, her face tipped toward us, though her eyes were blindfolded and hands bound by gossamer cloth. An intricate design carved a circle into the floor around her.

"Brogan?" she asked. "Lula?"

"Yes," Lula breathed, not moving any closer to the circle that licked with smoke.

This was a trap. We knew it. The Hush had told us so.

"Give me a minute," Val said. He and his wolf floated a circumference around the chamber.

I touched Lu's arm. "Val."

She nodded.

"I can't see you," Abbi said. "I thought I could get Hado free. But they had threads. I don't like their threads." She scowled and a watery white glow radiated around her.

"They watch," Thrum said. "Faster. Free her faster."

The hunters pulled up on either side of us.

"What's the hold up?" Elmer griped.

"Thrift store man?" Abbi asked. "Are you angry? I promise I won't bring trouble to your store."

"If I cared about that, I wouldn't have yelled about it," Elmer said. "Looks like a demon trap. Didn't think a demon trap could hold a Moon Rabbit. You stuck, Moon Bunny?"

"Oh, no, I'm not trapped. But if I cross the spell lines, the gates of darkness open. Then the Hush will devour the land and blot out the sky. So." She shrugged, and looked very much like a child bored with explaining the mystical as the mundane.

"Is that true?" I asked Thrum.

"Why do you think I've thrown in with you against the Mother, *broken heart*? I have reasons to want the darkness to remain where it is. I have reasons not to want more Hush upon the land."

"Or blotting out the sky," Abbi reminded him.

"Yes," he said, "or that."

"I can't see any magic holding her," Val said.

"I just said there isn't," Abbi complained. "Just that demon spell. But Hado is caught. There's a hook thing."

I lifted my flashlight, we all did, trying to find Hado. I didn't think we'd have much luck since he was a Shadow and, in a cave this deep, there was nothing but shadows.

Then I saw something move, a darker shape in the darkness. Two cool moon-gray eyes glowed back at me, standing nearly my height.

"Hado?" I asked.

He shifted, and I could see the hook Abbi was talking about. It looked like a scythe, the shine of it disappearing into the meat of him before curving up through him like an oversized darning needle.

A chain connected the hook to the floor, leaving him barely enough slack to stand.

I took a step, just as Thrum called, "She is here!"

An explosion of light spread across the walls, blindingly bright. When I could see again, the ceiling was undulating with bodies. The Hush hissed and clacked, moving fast down the curve of the walls on silver strings, skittering on shadowy feet.

Fear and anger spiked through the connections that tied us, and the answering mental howl of every were-wolf nearly brought me to my knees.

We are coming, we are coming, we are coming, the voices promised, as the connections grew stronger, tighter.

"*This now,*" Mother Hush's voice sang from the darkness, "*this, your slow and rotting death. This, your final breath.*"

The Hush were fast, but Elmer was faster.

The old guy shouldered his gun, taking aim at the ceiling. "Run!"

I ran toward Abbi, Lu a step ahead of me.

Elmer squeezed the trigger. The clap of sound was agony in the enclosed space.

I yelled, but couldn't hear my own voice over the ringing in my ears.

Abbi's mouth fell open in a surprised "O," and Hado lunged against the hook and chain that held him to the stone floor, trying to put himself between Abbi and the monsters falling from the ceiling.

Except the monsters weren't falling. Elmer fired off another shot, and a thick haze of smoke clouded the ceiling and filled the chamber.

No, not smoke. Rooroo dust.

"Out!" Josie yelled, her mouth at my ear. She hucked a glass jar against the floor, and it burst, sending more dust into the air.

The chamber filled with the blood-chilling screams of the Hush.

Lu reached Abbi before me, pulling her forward across the demon circle. As soon as Abbi crossed, copper fire burned through the spellwork, and thunder rolled beneath our feet.

That wasn't good. Couldn't possibly be good.

I grabbed the silver hook caught in Hado's shadowy form.

The hook burned cold in my grip. I yelled and yanked on the Hush-forged metal with numb hands.

Hado snarled, more cat than man. I pressed my hand against his side—his muscles clenched beneath soft, velvet fur—and shoved, sliding the hook out at the same time.

Hado howled and sprinted away, running after Abbi, running after Lu.

I was frozen. I couldn't release the hook, had no control over my own hands.

The voices in my head crashed, too many wolves, too many hunters, too many connections.

The Hush gibbered and shrieked.

The world was a rock tumbler, and I was nothing but sand.

My vision narrowed, and what light I could see seemed to be far, far away.

Lu, I whispered, as consciousness slipped.

"Move, move, move!" Lu slapped the hook out of my hand. Blood gushed warm and slick over my palms. She yanked my arm over her shoulder and dragged me out of the demon circle, half-walking, half-stumbling.

The air was thick with Rooroo dust and fangs.

That's when I realized the werewolves had arrived.

We stumbled, eyes stinging with darkness and dust. The snarl of werewolves, the flash of fang and claw rolled and shifted around us.

Once, I thought a Hush had found a way through the dust, had found a way through the ocean of fury and fur, but it was swept away by the dagger in Pamela's hand, which appeared, then disappeared as she pivoted to stay with the battle.

"We should—" I tried to slow, to tell Lu that we needed to help them, to fight.

"Here," she said, as we rounded a bend, the fight behind us. She let go of my arm, and bent toward something.

I blinked hard to clear my eyes. Not something, someone.

Abbi.

Lu worked to untie Abbi's arms. I reached into my pocket for the Rooroo dust shaker, but my pocket was empty.

Shit.

Then I remembered I had the lightning rod hooked onto my belt. I pulled it and hissed as metal hit raw flesh. I switched it to my other hand.

"We need to get her out of here," I said. "Take her. Go."

"Still not leaving you behind, Gauge." Lu threw the bindings on the ground and gently pulled the blindfold from Abbi's eyes.

"You can't stay," Abbi said. "Mother Hush wants to kill you, Brogan. She wants to eat you—your magic."

Lu grabbed my sleeve. "We go together." She clicked

on her flashlight, but the dust reflected the light back at us like a wall.

"This way," Abbi said, pulling on my other sleeve.

I followed, Lu bringing up the rear. I thought I could hear the soft growl of Hado moving in front of Abbi, but he was invisible in the dark.

We were climbing. Every once in a while the sound of the fight would rise, but after a few turns in the pathway, the struggle was muffled by stone.

I knew we were getting closer to the surface—the texture of grit beneath our feet changed, became thicker, as if stone had been broken here, worn down by animals or perhaps humans brave enough to enter.

I could smell the clear air, just a whiff at first, lost again when we trudged up and around another turn.

"Oh," Abbi said. "I can hear it. I can feel it. Can you feel it? The sky!" She released my sleeve and somehow had the energy to run up the incline.

"Abbi," Lu called, and then she put on speed and jogged up the hill.

I tried to pick up the pace, but like a bellows with a hole in it, each breath came harder and did less.

One turn I could see the glow of red from the dagger Lu carried, and the next, I was faced with three tunnels, all dark, all deserted.

I'd lost them. Lost my way.

I settled my breathing as best I could and focused on finding Ricky in the clamor of connections.

The war being waged between werewolf and Hush strained and snarled the connections, making them all light up with jagged pops of color that tangled and flared.

I could feel Ricky, that solid violet string above me in the clear air, beneath the clear sky, but I couldn't tell which of these three tunnels would lead me through the twists and turns to her.

I thought, *maybe the narrow one on the right*, and almost ducked into it.

The Hush were there blocking the tunnel, some of them burnt and leaking fluid, some of them missing limbs and eyes.

All of them hungry and moving my way.

I scrambled backward, and the tunnels were gone, closed by the same mechanism Thrum had used, leaving nothing but smooth stone where there had just been a promise of escape.

I could still feel Ricky's violet thread and knew there was another way out.

I spun.

In front of me rose Mother Hush.

"I will always find you, BroGan Gaayge. Devour you, hands and voice. Mine, now. Mine."

Mother Hush hinged upward, a towering monstrosity of nightmare, of evil.

I raised the lightning rod, but no magic answered.

She struck, spider fast, her razor fingers slashing.

I stumbled back and twisted, blocking the avalanche of blows out of desperation, unable to focus my will on the weapon, unable to trigger its magic.

I put my back to the wall. A heavy claw slammed into the side of my head and my knees went soft. My skin felt stung by a million pricks, cold threads from her needled fingers hooking into me, draining my strength.

Mother Hush drew up to her full height, clicking and hissing, tugging the threads she'd sewn into my skin.

I was still standing, barely, but didn't have the strength to raise my arms.

Ricky's mark burned hot against my hand. With each pulse, the connections flared.

A howl of *family* and *fight* and *protect*—werewolves.

A shout of *attack* and *guard* and *stand*—hunters.

Brighter than all the others: *anger* and *home* and *love love love*—Lula.

All of them, a part of me. All of us, one. I drew on them, calling on that power, that magic, that love. It rushed through me, screaming, thundering, a rock tumbler crash of *life life life*.

The lightning rod exploded with power.

Mother Hush opened her mouth wide, a huge maw of jagged teeth.

And then Val was there, at my side.

"Don't," I said, not knowing what he was going to do, but not wanting to lose him.

"Lu would kill me if I didn't save you," he said. "Like I want to die twice."

Everything happened too fast, and yet agonizingly slow.

I pulled back the lightning rod, fueling it with the fury, the roar, the chaos of *love love love and life life life*—

—Val leaped into me—

—*loyalty, hatred, kill kill kill*—

—Val launched out of me, diving into the lightning rod—

—just as I hurled it with all my strength—

—adding his spirit, his soul into the weapon.

"No!" I yelled, reaching for Val, trying to grab his spirit. But the ghost slipped through my fingers, lost in the weapon's magic.

Mother Hush lunged, jaws snapping.

Too late. Much too late.

The lightning rod struck true, impaling the creature through the throat. Her head whipped back, hands scrabbling at the metal stake, her scream beyond the range of human hearing.

The lightning rod exploded with Crossroad magic that tore through Mother Hush like a wildfire through brittle trees.

All our hatred, all our anger, all our fear fed that magic. Bolstering it, like a jet engine beneath a wing, was trust, friendship, love.

Unbreakable.

Mother Hush whipped and spiraled in a final macabre dance, burning alive, consumed. Then the magic detonated.

I covered my head, the explosion deafening, blinding, but nothing fell on me except dust and ash.

Mother Hush was gone.

The lightning rod was gone.

The connection to Ricky's magic was gone, leaving me cold and shivering.

"Val?" I asked, looking for him in the darkness.

I braced one hand on the wall behind me and closed

my eyes, reaching out for the ghost, for any fragment of him that might still exist.

"You get your ass over here and possess me right now," I growled.

Nothing.

"I'm not going back without you."

Nothing.

"Please, Val," I whispered.

Then, the slightest brush of coolness, a nudge too exhausted for more.

I opened my eyes and saw Val's wolf, burned, its eyes swollen shut, its breathing ragged.

My heart caught.

"There you are," I said softly. "We need to go now."

The wolf whined and dropped his head.

"No, you're coming with me. Don't you dare give up now. You have family, Val. Ricky, Danube. Lu and I, we're your friends. We're your family, if you'll have us."

The wolf took one shaky step. I opened my arms, pulling him closer.

When I was a spirit, I was a doorway for ghosts. I knew how to straddle the plane of their existence and the living world.

Just because I was a part of the living world didn't mean I'd forgotten how to accept a ghost, how to allow myself to be that doorway.

The wolf leaned forward. I pulled him into me, shivering now at the strangeness of sharing my living flesh with an unliving spirit. "I got you," I said. "I'll carry you home."

"Brogan!" Lu called from behind me.

Then she was there, helping me to my feet, and I was telling her I was fine, I was fine, we were fine.

We walked the dark pathway, her arm around me, pulling me up and up. We breached the surface, gulped down the shocking freshness of an open sky, and fell, gratefully, into the embrace of friends. Surrounded. Safe.

CHAPTER SEVENTEEN

I felt the cold of the truck's tailgate behind my thighs, remembered lying on the blanket someone had spread, Lorde curled beside me, her big fuzzy head on my stomach.

I saw the sky, dark and pricked through with clean white holes.

I heard voices, someone trying to talk Ricky into the passenger seat, someone growling softly, someone whining.

Lu was there, would always be there, settling herself so that my head was on her lap, her hands in my hair.

"It's okay, it's okay, it's okay," she kept saying, a tremble in her voice I hadn't heard for a long time. Fear. It was fear.

And then I heard Abbi.

"I think I should close the door," she said conversationally. "We don't want them coming out of there. So maybe I'll just…um…lock it."

"Don't you dare go toward that cavern," Lu called, and several of the werewolves growled louder.

I could hear a commotion.

"Lu," I said. "Love, let me… Lu, let me up."

She pressed my shoulder and scowled, looking down at me with stars in her hair.

I smiled. "Gods, you're beautiful."

She shook her head. "I'm annoyed with you. You need to rest."

"I'm—"

"If you say 'fine' one more time, I will poke one of your wounds."

"—fine. Ow!"

She raised an eyebrow. "Do I need to poke another one to make my point?"

"Just, no, yes, all right. I am not fine. There? Good? Can I sit up now, which I feel perfectly capable of, and if I am incorrect on that matter, you can tell me you told me so?"

Her honey eyes glowed in the darkness, and it was all I could do not to card my fingers into her hair and kiss her.

"I want to see Abbi. Please."

She shifted back so I could get my hands under me and lever up. My head swam, but the dizziness passed quickly.

Abbi was surrounded by werewolves. No, not just Abbi. Her Shadow was there too.

I blinked. "I'm seeing a huge black panther, right?"

Lu placed her hand on my back to steady me. "You are. That's Hado."

"What are they arguing about?"

"She wants to close the doors into the caverns."

"She's not going back in there."

"I know. I told her that. They're not going to let her. You should lie down."

"I don't have to go to the door," Abbi said. "I can just stand right here and do it, but you need to step back or you might get burned."

The werewolves looked doubtful, but finally, Danube nodded. "All right, little bunny, just don't get any closer to the cave."

She grinned, and the hulking panther moved to stand closer to her. "Hado. Do you have it?"

The panther huffed and opened his mouth, dropping something into her waiting hand.

"Oh, good!" she chirped. "I thought we lost it." She scrubbed fingers over the panther's ears, then held the object to the sky.

"Box?" I asked.

Lu, with her better eyesight said, "Pestle and mortar."

"Huh."

Abbi drew the little stick and bowl toward her face and whispered to it, while grinding the pestle against the bottom of the bowl, as if pulverizing her words.

Moonlight, white as softened snow filled the container, then grew and grew until the dark, moonless night brightened.

Abbi said one more musical word, then the light in the mortar flew across the street, through the bushes and trees, to the hill and cavern beyond.

Even with my poor eyesight, I could make out the silver moonlight forming into ropes, vines, crawling over the cavern's entrance. It glowed bright enough that I had to turn my eyes away and blink until I could see again.

The night was dark, more so than before.

"There," Abbi said. "That will hold."

"How long?" Elmer asked.

"As long as I want it to." Abbi slumped back against the panther, half burying her face in his fur. "A long time," she said, "for what they did to him."

His purr was loud, as he allowed her to hug him, then he butted her with his head, and she reluctantly released him.

"How can we help you, Moon Rabbit?" Summer asked. "Would you come home with us now?"

"Or with us," Cove offered.

"I'll decide later," Abbi said. "We should all go back to Ricky's house now. She has food and warm water for baths."

"I do," Ricky said, sounding more tired than I'd ever heard her. "And medicines, for those who need them."

It didn't take long to get everyone who wasn't in wolf form loaded into the vehicles. Lu stayed with me in the back of Silver, and so did Lorde.

Pamela offered to drive, and Lu agreed, which surprised me.

"What?" Lu asked, as she handed Pamela the keys.

"You love this truck."

"I love you more."

I opened my mouth to tease her, but she gave me a

look, and I decided it had been a long hard night for all of us.

I must have drifted off before we got back to the Crossroads. I dreamed I was a ghost, a wolf, running free in a summer forest, looking for a path, a way through the trees. I dreamed I was looking for my family, looking for a way home.

I woke to Lu's fingers skating down my cheek. "We're here."

Lorde rested her fuzzy head down on my stomach again and sneezed on me.

Lu rubbed the dog's head. "Come on, Lorde, let's get all of us inside and wash the dust off. Brogan?"

"I'm awake," I said, though I was still reaching for the dream. There was something important there, something I needed to remember.

The bathing took some time. Hunters each took their turn in the showers, and so did Lu and I. I offered to help bathe Lorde, but Lu shooed me off to the great room where we were all supposed to gather.

The werewolves bathed outside using the hot water hose set up, most of them naked in human form and completely comfortable with that.

I rested on the love seat as the great room slowly filled with people. Abbi and Hado wandered in, then the hunters, and Lu, who sat with me in the love seat. The werewolves arrived in noisy crowds.

Ricky finally rambled into the room carrying a whiskey bottle with a strip of masking tape that read "Apple Cider" slapped over the label, and a few brushes in her other hand.

The air charged with a tingling sensation as soon as she set the items on a side table.

"Shortest way to break what's left of the bonds, though there'll be a bit of a sting." Ricky opened the bottle, releasing the scent of apple cider and rosemary into the room.

She fingered a small needle out of her cuff and poked the tip of her finger.

She dipped the brush into the tipped bottle, swiped the wet bristles over the bead of blood, and rolled her hand open to reveal a tattoo of a padlock on the inside of her wrist. "You all might want to take a nice deep breath and think happy thoughts."

Before I could catch a breath, she slashed the brush over the lock tattoo.

There was a *click*, a burst of lavender light, and a pinch of pain.

Heartbeats I'd become accustomed to were gone. The voices, the emotions, the strangely comforting chaos of two wolf packs, a handful of hunters, and a single Crossroad, gone.

I exhaled like the air had been slapped out of me. Lu did the same.

A few of the wolves growled, others whined, and then they all drew toward each other, drew toward Summer and Cove, touching, arms around shoulders, hands catching hands, wolf bodies leaning against legs.

Pack. Family.

Lu rested her head on my shoulder, soft breath warm on the exposed skin of my neck.

We stayed like that for some time. Until the beat of

her heart and mine were once again in rhythm, until the connection between us, which had never broken, which even death couldn't strip away, filled the space abandoned by dozens of broken bonds.

Until we were once again, just us.

"It's going to be okay," Abbi said, though I didn't know which of us she was talking to. "I'll go make some more moon balls."

Abbi and her panther went into the kitchen, and half a dozen wolves detached from the hug-fest to flank them like a royal guard.

"Did everyone get out?" Lu asked.

Ricky's coloring looked off, dark circles smeared beneath her eyes. She nodded. "Which is a damn miracle. I thought I'd lost some of you fools. Haven't seen Val, though."

I shivered as echoes of the dream drifted through me. "He saved me," I said. "He sacrificed himself."

"Did he stay behind?" Ricky asked, confused. "I don't feel his loss." She pressed her fingers, one of which now had a bandage on it, against the TV tattoo on the side of her neck. "My connection to him isn't broken."

"He was badly hurt." I braced for the next bit. "I… uh…might have let him possess me. Might have insisted on it."

Lu pulled away so she could stare at me. "You let him possess you?"

I frowned. "He wasn't walking out of there on his own."

"So you let him possess you. A ghost. Valentine. You let Valentine possess you."

"If I say yes again, will you stop asking me the same thing?"

She smiled, a big, beautiful thing. "You like him."

I scowled harder, but it wasn't doing any good against that glimmer in her eyes. "I like him enough not to want him dead. Deader," I corrected.

"Is he still with you?" she asked.

"I don't feel any different. I think I dreamed about him. His wolf."

"Well, this is a switch." She pressed her palm against my sternum. "Usually you're the one pulling ghosts out of me."

"Oh, I can call him out," Ricky said. "But first, I need a cup of coffee. It's been a long damn night." She pushed to get out of the chair and was pressed back down by several wolves.

Pamela announced, "Josie, Elmer, we're on kitchen duty. Let's see what we can pull together for a meal. You stay right there, Crossroads. I'll send Elmer out with your coffee in a minute."

"Do I look like a butler?" Elmer grumbled.

Josie snorted. "You look like a grouchy old man." She pushed him down the hall after Pamela. "He'll be out in a minute," she said with a wink over her shoulder. "He might even be wearing a suit and tie."

"I don't own a suit and tie, and furthermore…" Whatever he said next was drowned out by Josie's laughter.

"Hunters are going to cook for us?" Summer asked, maybe more to herself than anyone else. Most of the werewolves in the room were staring after Elmer.

"Yes?" Cove suggested. "Unless Ricky has werewolf poison in the kitchen?"

Werewolf heads swiveled toward Ricky.

"Well, not in the kitchen," Ricky replied.

I smiled at the instant swivel of wolf heads to their leaders.

"She's joking." Abbi walked into the room with a carafe and a box propped on her hip. She set them both down on a table near the window and unpacked cups, cream, and sugar.

"I made coffee." She smiled at Ricky and handed her a mug.

"Thank you." She had the cup to her lips almost before she got the last word out. She gulped down at least half the cup, and her shoulders dropped.

The strain of being the focal point for all the connections so far from her place of power—her home —showed in the pallor of her skin and the slight shake of her hands.

It had taken a lot out of her.

"All right, Brogan," she gestured to me, "let's get Valentine where he belongs."

Abbi handed me a mug and shook her head just slightly.

I lifted the mug toward Ricky. "If you don't mind, I think I'll drink this coffee first."

If Ricky knew what I was doing, she went with it, leaning her head against the chair and setting her cup on the table. "If you must."

She was snoring softly before Abbi returned with the next carafe of coffee and didn't rouse until we'd all eaten our fill of the biscuits and gravy the hunters cooked up.

Morning was only a couple hours away now, but, as Ricky had said, it had been a long damn night.

Without much conversation, we all drifted off to different rooms to sleep, Abbi curled up on the couch in the living room with Hado at her feet. Someone found a thick blanket and draped it over Abbi. Both wolf packs stayed in the room, tucking into spaces and each other's arms.

Lu took me by the hand to the bedroom I considered ours now, the temptation of warm blankets and soft bed too much to resist.

"Do you know where the hunters are?" I asked.

"They took two of the bedrooms," Danube's voice said from just outside our half-open door. "Are you going to be okay here?" he asked.

I didn't know if he was worried about us or about Valentine.

"We're fine," Lu said, which was good because I was yawning.

"If you need anything," he said, "I'll be right outside the door." He stepped away, though I didn't know how far.

"What are we going to do about Abbi?" she asked, pulling the pillows where she wanted them and straightening the old quilts over us.

"What should we do?" I asked, half asleep already.

"That's what I'm asking you. What should we do?"

"I think," I said, my words thick, "we're going to ask her what she wants, and that's what we'll make happen."

I listened to Lu breathing, listened to the house settle and creak, the almost audible hum of Ricky's magic wards simmering in the air. It was strangely quiet now that all the connections had been broken, and my thoughts were just my own.

I should feel happy about it, but there was a part of me that missed the chaos, the clamor, the vitality of being a part of something so much more than myself.

I lay there, wondering what the werewolves were dreaming, wondering what roads the hunters followed in their slumber until sleep came down the corridor and punched my ticket.

CHAPTER EIGHTEEN

"Have you decided yet?" Summer asked Abbi.

Dawn was coming on sweet, the greens greener, the breeze cooler, the sun a buttery softness amongst bird song.

It was the sort of day that made one want to watch it bloom.

It was the sort of day that made one itchy to hit the road, to travel that old pathway, searching for answers to old questions.

Where were the monsters who had nearly killed us all those years ago? Where was the spell book of the gods? Where was our tomorrow?

"I think so," Abbi said. She sat on the porch railing, swinging her feet. Her Shadow was out in the grass and trees, running with the wolves.

Summer rested her hand on Abbi's head. "You're not staying with us, are you?"

Ricky strode out onto the porch, looking her normal self—which is to say smug and annoying—after the three hours of sleep she'd gotten. Today she was wearing a pair of overalls covered in hand-painted frogs.

"Brogan, I was looking for you. I think it's time to find Valentine."

My heart lurched, and Lu, who was out by the truck putting in supplies for our travels, looked back at me.

I gave her a wave. "All right," I said. "Here?"

One of the wolves had chased the panther up the tree, and now a mob of them were circling and yipping, tails wagging. Lorde was out there in the thick of it, having the time of her life.

The panther yowled and hissed at them.

Forget the pretty soft morning. It was noisy as hell.

"Inside." Ricky nearly shouted to be heard.

I followed her down a narrower side hall. She opened a bright yellow door, and we stepped into a room lit by four skylights and decorated with a hodge-podge of antiques, DIY projects, and handmade pieces.

A day bed, a tiny corner desk, a small gray couch furnished the room, and, adding a punch of color, a yellow velvet chair that matched the door.

I dropped onto the couch and was surprised at the room's silence.

"Don't hear that?" Ricky asked. "I had it sound-proofed years ago. After a group of banshees decided to stay for a few months to work out some differences. Screamed when they were angry, screamed when they were sad. Screamed when they were happy. What I'm saying is, it was a lot of screaming. This was the only way I could get some sleep."

"Are you expecting them back?"

"Who knows?" She sat in the yellow chair. She was big enough to hide most of the color from my line of sight. "All sorts of people show up here, and I do what I can to help them, or," she made ocean-wave motions with one hand, "move them along."

"Did you help the banshees or move them along?"

She grinned, and those dimples popped. "Well, they got over their differences."

I leveled at look at her, and she chuckled. "It was a misunderstanding. As soon as I tricked them—I mean *assisted in their agreement*—" She winked. "—they finally listened to what the others were saying and realized they had been wanting the exact same thing, just going at it from different angles. Also, I might have bound them with truth spells for a week."

My eyebrows shot up. "Did you tell them you were using magic on them?"

She shrugged. "Details. It all turned out happily ever after. So, let's talk about Valentine. You said he was hurt?"

"Yes. His wolf. He was hurt."

"All right. Let's see what we see." Ricky pressed her finger to the TV tattoo. "I need to talk to you, Valentine. Here. Right here."

A tug in my chest behind my sternum, and also, an echoing tug in my head, made me close my eyes and exhale slowly.

"I can't quite…" Ricky said. "You need to speak up, Val. I can't quite hear you."

I thought I heard a faint howl, thought I tasted the sun-warmed loam of a forest floor. The tug on my bones flared hot, burning me from the inside. Sweat broke over my face, soaked the back of my shirt, and trickled down my sides.

"Okay, now I see you," Ricky said, "you're doing great. Keep reaching. Purple. Look for the purple."

The heat cranked up, then it was gone, leaving prickling relief behind.

My muscles felt heavy, like I'd just sprinted up a few dozen flights of stairs.

"I… I hear you," Val said. "Ricky. I'm here."

Ricky shifted in the chair and looked to her right. "Welcome back, Val."

Valentine was more transparent than usual. Scrapes and bruises darkened his skin and he looked like he'd just shaken loose of a nightmare he couldn't remember. His wolf was with him, just the barest flash of eyes and fur.

"I can't." Val frowned and squeezed the back of his neck. "I can't remember."

"You were in a fight with a Hush," Ricky said. "Do you remember that?"

"We were in the caverns," he said, his hand still on his neck. "Brogan. She was going to kill him."

"You stopped her," I said. "You saved me, Valentine. Thank you."

His gaze skittered, then homed in on me. "Hey, Brogan."

Ricky leaned forward and carded her fingers together. Soft purple glowed between them. "Are you ready to move on, Val? There's a light for you. A place for you that is much kinder than here."

Val squared off to the Crossroads. He dropped his hand from his neck and crossed his arms over his chest. "Did you just give me the it's-okay-to-die speech? Are you trying to get rid of me? Who put you up to this? Was it Danube? I am so going to haunt his ass."

Ricky smiled, just a slight twitch at the corners of her mouth, but I felt my shoulders relax and my pulse settle. Val was fine, or he would be fine.

I didn't want to admit how much relief washed through me.

"I was giving you options," Ricky said.

"You were trying to evict me from this mortal realm."

"Which is an option."

"Did I ask for options?"

"Crossroads here, remember? All about dishing out the happy times."

"You think dying, again, *more*, would make me happy?"

"Not having to hear you complain would make me happy," I muttered.

Ricky snorted.

"You," Val said, "can stay all the hell out of this."

There was a knock on the door.

"Well, if you're not walking into the light today," Ricky stood, "you are officially back in the good old messed up world of the living. Congratulations on that stellar decision. You are welcome to stay here with me a while. As long as you want."

Val looked over at me. "What's everyone else doing? The packs? Abbi? You and Lu?"

"Everyone's leaving, I think. Lu and I will be gone today."

"Oh." It was just one word, but it carried a punch of disappointment, of sorrow.

"Abbi wanted to talk to you, Ricky," Danube said from the door. "Talk to all of us. I told her I'd find you. Everything okay? Is Valentine okay?"

Val wasn't watching me anymore, his attention wholly on Danube, and there was a longing there that I didn't think he was aware of. Maybe staying and working out whatever was to be worked out with Danube would be the best thing for the ghost.

I stood and managed not to groan at all my aches.

"He's back," I said. "I have a feeling he might be staying for a bit."

Val threw a look my way and nodded.

"But he's still getting his feet under him. Might need some time to heal," I added.

"Here?" Danube said, as I gestured for Val to proceed me through the door. "Will he be staying here to heal?"

"Would you like that?" Ricky asked, as she stepped out with all of us into the narrow hall and shut the door.

I could see the conflict on Danube's face before his expression settled into a weary acceptance.

"I know Val's listening," Danube said. "If I say I'd really like him to stay, is that just going to push him away? Because I want to say the thing that makes him stay."

Ricky and I both looked at Val. He dropped his gaze to stare at his shoes and said nothing.

"Of all the times for him to shut up," I sighed. "Look. I think he's going to make his decision soon, and we're going to have to give him time to do it. And I think everything's going to be all right eventually. Everyone's going to get over their stubborn hurt feelings, and work out their misunderstandings like adults."

Danube's hands curled into loose fists, then he nodded. "That sounds good," he said. "That sounds… yeah. I'd like that."

"Okay," I said.

"Okay," he said.

Val didn't say anything, but when Danube turned and started down the hall toward the rest of the people in the house, Valentine drifted at his side, close, but not touching.

"You know," Ricky said, "that was pretty inspired."

"Don't start."

"I mean, I might have taken a run at it eventually, but you cut right through that crap and got them thinking. You ever consider doing this for a living?"

I scoffed and started down the hall.

"Plenty of room here for you and Lu, and it's not like I don't have a million repair projects I've been meaning to get to. Put those big shoulders of yours to use. Take out your rage on some sixteen-penny nails and that shop I've been meaning to frame."

"Who says I have rage?"

"Oh, Brogan," she said quietly from where she walked behind me. "That weapon I gave you? The rod?"

I didn't answer, not sure I was ready to hear what she was going to say.

"It isn't just will that calls magic into it. It's brutal, raging fury."

"You couldn't have told me that?" I asked.

"I was pretty sure I didn't need to, because I was pretty sure you had more than enough rage—at the Hush, at the gods, at the world—to fuel it. Was I right?"

I stopped before we exited the hall to the rest of the house and turned to face her. "It wasn't rage," I said. "Or, it wasn't just rage. It was more than that."

She waited, brown jasper eyes calm.

"It was love." I wanted to look away, but she touched my arm, and I didn't flinch, didn't feel the need to pull away from her warm, steady contact. "My love," I said, "and well, all of ours. Together."

Her smile was crooked, and she looked pleased with me. "Yep," she said, "it was all that too."

CHAPTER NINETEEN

The wolves sprawled in skin or fur across the lawn, the two packs separated but more comfortable in each other's space than they had been even a day ago.

The binds that Ricky had given us had left their mark. We had gone to battle together, had saved the Moon Rabbit and Shadow together. In some ways, we would always be a part of each other.

The trio of hunters stood to one side below the porch. Every now and then a wolf would call something out to them, there would be an answer, and everyone would laugh.

I shook my head. Hunters were not friends. Not to monsters like werewolves, not to monsters like Lu and me.

Still, I couldn't help but be grateful that Elmer, Pamela, and Josie had thrown their lot in with us, at least this once, against the Hush.

I didn't know if I could count on them in the future, but I was glad to know them in this now.

Lu shifted next to me on Silver's tailgate. Lorde had abandoned us to sit with the Riggs, her tongue lolling as she got all the petting and scratching she could desire.

Abbi and her panther also lounged in the grass. Ricky remained sitting on the top step of her porch. A flicker of light near her resolved into Valentine, who sat on the top step too.

"All right, Abbi," Danube said, strolling out onto the grass to sit with the Riggs. "We're all here. Drop the bomb."

She smiled, and even after all we'd been through, that smile was pure and sweet.

"I know you all love me," she said. A couple of the weres grumbled their disagreement, and she wrinkled her nose. "You do," she laughed. "I'm a part of the moon, and you love *love* the moon.

"Also, you helped me find Hado. That was…" Her voice fell out from under her, and suddenly she looked much, much older, and much, much sadder. "…that was everything to me. You didn't have to help me, but you did. Thank you." The last came out as a whisper.

Hado wrapped his fluffy tail closer around her, and even from our distance, I could hear his purr.

"I want to spend more time with you. All of you. Both packs," she added. "But not right now."

Summer and Cove shook their heads. "You need to be with us, Abbi," Summer said. "We kept you safe and will keep you safe. Just because you sealed up one cavern doesn't mean there aren't more caverns. More Hush."

"Or worse things," Cove said.

"Of course there's worse out there," Elmer said. "There always is."

There was more murmuring from the wolves, and I was giving it fifty-fifty odds they'd try to kidnap her and the panther to keep her safe.

"You could stay with me," Ricky said, her voice strong, but somehow blending in with the place, as if the grass, the trees, and the blue sky itself were a part of it. "Always room for one," she glanced at Val, "or two more."

The wolves liked this idea, but Abbi was already shaking her head.

"I don't think I should stay. Not now. Not for a little while." She stood and walked our way.

Hado yawned, stretched, and followed her.

"Uh, oh," I said quietly to Lu.

"Hi, Brogan," Abbi said when she was close enough.

"Abbi," I said.

"Hi, Lula." She stopped just a couple feet away from us. Close enough I could see the crease between her eyes, the twisting of her fingers with her other fingers.

Lorde had followed behind both of them, sniffing at Hado, who ignored her completely.

"Hello, Abbi," Lula said. "What's up?"

"I just told all the werewolves I'm leaving."

"I heard that," Lu said.

"They're still worried about me, but I'm not. Worried about me." She tugged her hands apart and stuck them behind her back.

"All right," I said. "What are you worried about?"

"I want you to take me with you." Her eyes flew

wide, and she slapped her hand over her mouth. Then she shrugged. "If you want."

"Why would you want to go with us?" Lu asked.

"I think I can help you."

"We don't need help, Abbi," Lu said.

"We really don't," I added, not wanting her anywhere near the dangerous waters we were headed into.

Abbi might not be a child, but she was kind. Hopeful. I didn't want to be a part of what broke that in her.

She leaned forward and pointed a finger at my lips. "I see the Hush threads sealing your lips. I can…" She wiggled her finger a little, her gaze steady on my mouth. "Break it."

"How?" I asked.

"It's a dream binding. I'm part of the moon, so dream stuff is sort of my thing."

Lu sensed my hesitation and rubbed her thumb over my wrist.

"All right," I said. "Please."

Hado gracefully lifted and planted both wide paws on the tailgate next to me, positioning himself next to Abbi. His gray eyes were smooth stones beneath clear cold river water.

She pulled her pestle and mortar out of her pocket and leaned forward, tipping up on the toes of her sneakers, her eyes bright and sharp. She whispered something across the mortar—a small verse that slipped in and out of my brain like a half-remembered lullaby—stirring her words with the pestle. Then she pressed the tip of her finger on my lips.

The threads snapped so suddenly, I inhaled through my nose, a great breath like I'd been unable to fill my lungs for days. Years.

Abbi studied my face, before she leaned back and looked at my chest, my arms and hands, and finally, my legs and feet. "I don't see any other strings. Do you feel any more?"

I shook my head. "No."

"Can you say what the Hush didn't want you to say?" Lu asked.

"Mother Hush wants me to find the book." My exhale was a little shaky, filled with the relief of being able to speak. "Return it to her, the Strange weave. That's what she called it."

"Strange weave," Val said, appearing on the other side of Lu. "Does that mean the whole book?"

He was growing more solid than when he'd first returned. His wolf was clearer too. But bruises still blackened his eyes, and scrapes, cuts, and bite marks reddened his skin.

"I've seen that book," Abbi said.

"Where?" Lu asked.

"Well, Earth," she said like that narrowed it down. Maybe it did, for a creature like her. "The Hush wanted it too. Wanted me to find it."

"Do you know where it is?" I asked.

"No, but I can hear it sometimes. I have really good ears, because, you know: rabbit. If I'm close enough, I'll hear it, no matter how well it's hidden."

So that was why Cupid wanted us to find her. That

was why the Hush had trapped her Shadow. They thought she'd find the book for them.

I still didn't like the idea of her getting mixed up in our promise to a god. But that same god had told us to do the right thing. Was leaving her behind right?

Danube wandered over, trying to make it look like he'd just decided to go for a stroll and had accidentally ended up at our truck.

"Hello, Lu. Brogan. Hello, Abbi."

Abbi rolled her eyes at him. "I'm going to miss you."

That admission stopped Danube dead in his tracks, his palms down and outward at either side, like he'd just realized he was walking a tightrope.

Val snorted, and Danube's gaze ticked that way, then back to Abbi.

"I'm going to miss you too," he said, putting his hands in his pockets and closing the distance. "Are you going to let her go with you?"

We hadn't had time to discuss it. Hadn't had time to decide if letting one more person into our life was what we needed or wanted.

But Lu nodded. "We can take her down the road a bit. For at least a little while. You're not going to help us find the book though, Abbi. That's our oath to fulfill, and we don't want to put you in danger." Lu held up her hand to stop Abbi's reply.

"When you decide you've been on the road enough and want something else, then you are free to follow that path. Without worrying about us. Okay?"

"Yes," Abbi said, the excitement fizzing off her like a shaken bottle of soda water. "I promise I'll let you know if I want to leave. And if I need help, I'll call on the Riggs and Kearneys. I know they'll hear me."

"We always will," Danube agreed.

"This is so exciting!" Abbi spun and trotted toward the house. "Crossroads. Can I pack some moon balls? I'm going on a road trip!"

"That is not how I thought we'd be continuing the journey," I said.

Lu shifted so she could look at me. "Did you want to say no? We still can."

"You know me, Lula." The breeze had strung a strand of auburn hair across her face. I slipped it back behind her ear. Her hand instantly came up to better secure her hair and to weave her fingers between mine.

"I trust you," I said. "If I think something needs more discussion, I'll say so."

She nodded, and I thought she secretly looked happy that Abbi would be with us for a while.

"What about Val?" Danube asked. He was still standing there, hands in his pockets, staring in Val's general direction. "Is he still here?"

"Tell him I'm still here," Val said.

"He's here," I dutifully supplied.

Danube's gaze found Val, even if he couldn't see him. "Is he going with you too? With Abbi? I wouldn't blame him," he said. "Tell him I wouldn't blame him."

"He can hear you," I said, while Val simultaneously said, "I still have ears, dumbass."

"Right," Danube said. "Well, are you? Going?"

Val scowled, and his hand dropped to his wolf, who leaned against his leg. "I don't think so." He looked up past Danube, over to Ricky, who was chatting with Elmer and Summer. Ricky must have cracked a heck of a joke at Elmer's expense because the old guy was bright red, and the other two were laughing their heads off.

"I think I'm going to stay."

The pang of loss, of sadness surprised me.

"He's staying," I said in half a voice. "Are you sure, Val?" I asked. "You know you can come with us."

The smile that spread on his face was pure delight. "Really, Brogan? Me? Are we buddies now?"

"No," I said. "I take it back. You should stay."

"You like me. Lu was right all along. You are dying to be my friend."

"I would rather chew old boots."

"You love me. You can't stand the idea of leaving me behind. We're friends, remember? *Family.* If I'll have you."

"You can keep him," I said to Danube. "Forever."

Danube's smile was small, but he nodded. "I want him to stay. If he wants. Somewhere around here, anyway."

"Right here," Ricky said, as she walked up. "He's already told me he'll haunt up my place for a bit.

"I've packed some food and a few extras, Lu, Brogan. Blankets, some clothing that should fit Abbi. Second hand, but good. Elmer picked those out."

We all looked over at Elmer with varying degrees of curiosity. He turned red again and dismissed us with a slash of his hand then stomped away to where Josie was chatting up a few of the Kearneys.

"And you can keep those boots, Brogan," Ricky said.

"That's good, because I wasn't gonna give them back."

Lu accepted the tote and pushed it into place in the truck bed. "He means thank you," she said.

Ricky snapped her fingers. "Before I forget. I noticed you've got a couple old postcards on the dash of your truck."

"Yeah?" I asked.

Lu narrowed her eyes.

"I'd like to buy one off of you."

"That so?" I asked. "Which one?"

"It's a 1948 inside view of Happy Hill Restaurant from up in Jerome. I got a buddy who collects that kind of thing."

"Interesting," I said, feeling smug. "How much you willing to pay for it?"

"I'll give you two-fifty because he's going to pay four-fifty, easy. It's a rare one."

I turned my grin on Lu. "You hear that, Lula? A rare one. Two-hundred fifty for the postcard. How much did you get for that bookmark?

Lu squinted at me.

"Oh, that was a good find too," Ricky said. "Pretty, with a little residual magic. But not worth as much as the postcard."

"Huh," I said. "Someone owes me a hotel room."

Lu planted her hands on her hips. "That bet's over. I still won."

"Really," I said. "Two-hundred fifty dollars says the bet's just been reopened, and a new winner has been declared."

"Could someone tell Val thank you for staying?" Danube said, cutting into our argument. "For me?"

"I'm not staying for him," Val said.

"Settle down," I said to Val. Then to Danube. "He heard you."

Val shifted his weight onto his back leg, trying to look relaxed. "I think I did what Cupid asked me to do, that's all."

"You did," I said.

"I got my chance at revenge. A chance to find out what really happened to me. I don't forgive the packs for what happened, but I think I understand. They didn't want me to die."

"No," Ricky said. "They didn't. Danube came to me back then. He tried to save you."

Danube had gone very still, his eyes glistening with what looked suspiciously like tears.

"We broke a demon trap down there in the caverns," Val went on. "Ricky thinks there might be some fallout from that. I thought I could help if there is."

"Oh, there will be," Ricky said.

"You need us to stay and deal with the demon trap?" I asked her.

"If I needed you to stay for every strange thing happening in these parts, Brogan Gauge, you and Lu would have to settle down here permanently."

"That's never going to happen," I said.

She grinned. "Scared you off with all that talk about building my shop, huh?"

"Nope. Just don't want to be talked to death by your current house ghost."

"Friendship revoked," Val said. "Have fun explaining to people why you're traveling across country with a child and a big-ass panther."

"Hope you stay here a long time, Val. A long, long time," I said. "Don't leave it on our account. Ever."

"Oh, I'll keep in touch," he said. "Ricky's gonna show me how I can use a cell phone, and I'll text you every day."

"I own a gun," I informed Ricky.

Lu's eyebrows rose. "He doesn't."

"Guns won't kill me," Ricky said conversationally. "Or Val. Just so you know."

"Maybe no one's found the right gun. It's all about the bullets, right?" I pressed. "Silver for werewolves."

"Careful," Danube warned.

"Salt won't hurt him," I muttered, "but I'm resourceful."

"Oh, ha-ha," Val said. "Like you could shoot me. I'm your best friend, Brobro."

Ricky opened her mouth in a huge smile, dimples popping. "Brobro?"

"Nope," I said. "Never use that name again."

"I think Brobro is kind of sweet," Ricky said.

I pointed a finger at her, which only made her laugh. "I hope you and Val are very happy with each other."

I pushed out of the truck bed and snapped my fingers softly for Lorde to follow, leaving the others chuckling behind me.

I strolled out to the trees to let Lorde do her business before we hit the road.

Elmer pushed off from the tree he was leaning on

and fell into step with me. "Suppose you'll be headed back down the road now," he said.

"I suppose," I said. "Thank you. For your help."

Elmer flicked his fingers, like none of that mattered. "Never have liked the Hush. Well, except for a handful of them. They used to keep to themselves, but they've been all riled up lately. Hungry. I couldn't make head or hind of it. But now I think it's something to do with you."

"Not sure how."

"Tied up with a god, friends with a ghost, not so sure what's alive and not alive about you, and there's the plain fact the Moon Rabbit wants to dog your steps. There's the other plain fact your wife wears an unholy key around her neck, and a ticker I haven't seen the likes of since I was in short pants. It stops time, doesn't it?"

"It can. You know something about the key? Said it's unholy?"

He shook his head, sunlight catching on the freckles and age spots on his thin skin. "Saw it on her neck when she was sitting with you in the truck last night. I know a magical thing when I see one. Know a cursed object."

"It's a key to a book," I said. "I suppose that's all you should know."

The grass brushed our ankles as we made our way toward one of the roads that bordered this place. Grasshoppers bounced out of our way, and honey bees lifted into the air before drifting down to ironweed and goldenrod blooms.

"You sure you don't want to tell me more? Might I could help."

"More likely it would just put you in danger," I said. "I'd hate to do that to a friend."

"A what now? What was that?" He cupped his ear and leaned toward me. "A friend?"

"Don't push it, hunter."

He cackled, and we turned back toward the house.

Abbi bounced down the porch steps, a bag of food balanced on her hip, talking at speed to her Shadow and the wolves who all surrounded her, hugging, touching, saying good-bye.

"I want your word you're not going to hurt any of those people," I said. "You or the other hunters in the area."

"If I'd wanted any of them harmed, it would have happened years ago. Naw, there's been a long standing peace. Might be on account of the Crossroads, might just be because these people aren't the monsters the old stories make them out to be."

I thought about the wolves in the darkness, tearing the guts out of the Hush, oily ichor spraying the walls of the cavern, blood lust in their eyes.

Monster might still fit.

But they were more than just killing machines. More than big bads to scare children. They were family, they were community, and they had shown they would protect those less powerful than they were.

"I'm seeing a few hunters in a different light," I admitted.

"Life is like that," Elmer said. "Shines a light on what you think you know. If you're lucky, you'll answer with your heart, instead of with all the stories people stuff in your head. Kindness is damn powerful. Any man who abides by it, changes the world. For the better, I'd say."

"Is that why you yelled Abbi and us out of your shop the other day?"

Elmer grimaced. "I'm not a perfect man. I was worried about her getting mixed up with you two. That girl trusts too easily."

"She's not a girl," I said, and he just made a sound that pretty much echoed my feeling.

She might be a hell of a lot older than Elmer, and even a hell of a lot older than me, but she was still inno-cent. I could see why he would want to make sure she wasn't trusting strangers rolling through his town.

She looked our way, as if she felt our gazes on her, and waved.

Lu laughed at the story Ricky and Danube were telling her, one that involved a lot of hand gestures. Even Val was getting in on the mime show.

"Looks like you've got a lot to look after now," Elmer said.

"Always have," I said, my gaze holding on Lu, until she finally looked up and gave me a quirk of her eyebrow. "Wouldn't trade that for the world."

"Good man," Elmer said. "I'm surprised to say it's been a pleasure to make your acquaintance, Mr. Gauge. Safe travels to you and yours." Elmer stuck out his knobby hand.

I accepted the gesture and returned the farewell so common on the road. "Safe travels."

"Oh, I'm not going anywhere," he said. "These old bones? I'm lucky I can get out of bed in the morning."

He tottered off, really playing up the old guy act, and I realized I was going to miss him too.

Being alive stirred up all kinds of emotions. But I was starting to enjoy feeling with my whole soul.

Lorde licked my fingertips, then walked with me back to Lu.

The werewolves drew out of my path like the tide retreating from the shore.

Ricky caught me in a hug I couldn't escape until I returned her hearty back slap and promised, really promised, that we'd be back soon. Next summer at the latest.

Danube shook my hand, but I drew him in closer so that our shoulders bumped. "Make things right with Val. He misses you and your friendship."

"I'll try," he said.

"See that you do. I'll be back by to check in. Don't tell Val I said that."

We loaded the last things into the truck. Lu swung into the driver's seat and adjusted the mirrors while I stood outside the open passenger door, Abbi and her huge panther next to me.

"Huh," I said. "I think he'll need to go in the back."

"What?" Abbi asked through a mouth full of moon balls. "Who?"

"Hado. There isn't room in the cab for all of us."

She glanced into the cab where Lu and Lorde had already claimed their space, then looked up at me.

"Oh, we'll be okay. Hado?"

She wiggled her fingers and tapped her shoulder.

Hado, the big black panther who could take down any of the strongest werewolves here, the Moon Rabbit's fierce protector who had fallen to earth and endured all manner of pain at the hands of the Hush to keep her safe, sneezed.

A poof of dark smoke filled my vision, then drifted off on the breeze.

Hado, the great protector, the mighty panther, was now a tiny black kitten.

He *mewed* in a tremulous voice, tipping his liquid gray eyes up at Abbi.

"Perfect!" She bent and scooped him up, plunking him on her shoulder where he settled down with a very tiny, self-satisfied, panther-like smirk.

That solved the problem of people noticing we were traveling with a huge black panther.

"Can we sit by the window?" Abbi asked.

"Sure." I swung up into the cab, Lorde shifting to put her head and paws on my thighs. She sighed happily, her ears twitching once, before she closed her eyes.

Abbi clambered up on my other side.

"Do you want me to shut the door?" I asked.

"I got it." She slammed the heavy door with ease.

Not a child, I reminded myself. *Not helpless*. Which was good. The road we traveled had never been easy. I didn't expect that to change.

She offered me the paper bag in her hand. "Do you want a moon ball? I ate all the ones with chocolate, but the plain ones are pretty good."

I shook my head, and she stared into the bag. "Oh, there's one more chocolate one!" She stuck her hand in, crumpling the paper as she tried to find her prize.

I draped my arm across the seat behind Lu.

She tugged her sunglasses out of the visor and settled them into place.

"Ready?" she asked.

"I am."

She put the truck into gear and aimed it toward the road. Werewolves and hunters raised their hands in farewell, and one ghost, shouted, "I'll see you soon, best friend, Brobro!" as we lurched off the gravel and onto the pavement.

"Does the radio work?" Abbi turned the knob.

The closing strains of a soft alto faded, and the DJ's voice came over the airwaves.

"This is KUPD, Missouri, keeping up with those kicks on Route 66. I'm Bo, and I'm sending out a song to a couple of crazy kids, crazy in love. They've been through some hard times recently, gotten themselves into some twists and turns, faced some setbacks. They didn't have a ghost of a chance against some of their troubles, but they never stopped fighting.

"I'm happy to say, with their sharp eyes, and sharper ears, they're on the road toward what I hope is success as they search for, well, all the good things we're searching for.

"Thanks for doing the right thing, Lu and Bro. This one's for you."

Abbi had gone very still, her hand hovering near the

dial. The song started, Cat Stevens' voice tumbling out, bright and hopeful.

Abbi looked over at us, old eyes in a young face. "That was Cupid."

"Yep," I said.

"So you really know him. Like *know him* know him."

I wasn't sure what that meant. "We've met him. More than once. He wanted us to find you."

She tipped her head. "Why?"

"He didn't tell us."

"Destruction," she said, "and connections. You helped me get Hado back. Connection. You helped us lock up the Hush. Destruction."

I squinted out the windshield, the day suddenly brighter, hotter, now that we were away from the Crossroads.

"I suppose," I said. "Maybe also for your sharp ears. Does it worry you? Us working for a god?"

"No," she said, "because he was just the start of it. We all have free will. Even the gods can't take that away."

Lu snorted. "Where have I heard that before?"

I smiled. "Some wise woman might have mentioned it once or twice. If I were a wiser man, I'd have listened to her."

Lu dropped her hand onto Lorde's soft fur. I brought my arm down so I could lace my hand with hers. "You're plenty wise enough for me," she said.

"Oh! It's our song, Hado!" Abbi started belting out lyrics, "…followed by…moon shadow…"

She got most of the words right but her pitch was

way off, too high, and swooping down to completely miss the next note.

Hado hid his face beneath the jagged brush of her white hair.

Abbi bounced carefully in the seat. At least she was on beat.

We had a lot of road ahead of us. Nothing was guaranteed. Not our journey, and certainly not how much time we had together. So I leaned over and kissed Lu on the cheek.

She glanced away from the road, her hand steady on the wheel, and gave me a smile that turned the world inside out.

"Love you," she said. This, our promise. Forever.

"Love you," I replied, as I always would.

Then I sat back and let the wild of the world—sky and hills, and the old ragged road—spool on by.

ABOUT THE AUTHOR

Devon Monk is a USA Today Bestselling writer of fantasy. Her series include Ordinary Magic, Souls of the Road, West Hell Magic, House Immortal, Allie Beckstrom, and Broken Magic. She also writes the Age of Steam steampunk series, and the occasional short story which can be found in her collection: A Cup of Normal, and in various anthologies.

She has one husband, two sons, and lives in lovely, rainy Oregon. When not writing, Devon is drinking too much coffee, watching hockey, or knitting silly things.

Want to read more from Devon?

Follow her blog, or sign up for her newsletter at: www.Devonmonk.com

Infinity Bell

Crucible Zero

BROKEN MAGIC

Hell Bent

Stone Cold

Backlash

ALLIE BECKSTROM

Magic to the Bone

Magic in the Blood

Magic in the Shadows

Magic on the Storm

Magic at the Gate

Magic on the Hunt

Magic on the Line

Magic without Mercy

Magic for a Price

AGE OF STEAM

Dead Iron

Tin Swift

Cold Copper

Hang Fire (short story)

SHORT STORIES

A Cup of Normal (collection)

Yarrow, Sturdy and Bright (Once Upon a Curse anthology)

A Small Magic (Once Upon a Kiss anthology)

Little Flame (Once Upon a Ghost anthology)

Wish Upon a Straw (Once Upon a Wish anthology)